Trust a Bedoowan?" Gaveth said. "I don't know."

For a second Alder thought he was joking. But he could see that the Milago boy was serious.

"Now!" Alder shouted.

"You don't have to yell," Gaveth said. He put his arms against the beam, braced himself, and heaved.

The beam slipped a little. But then it jammed on something and wouldn't move.

The quig was now clearing the rim of the shaft. In only seconds it would be on them.

"Never mind!" Alder shouted. "Run!"

They turned and ran with all their strength.

But they didn't get far. Alder's stomach sank as he saw what was in front of them. A blank wall.

"No!" Gaveth shouted. "No!" He pounded his fist against the rock.

Behind them there was a scraping noise and a thud. The two boys turned to look. The quig was in the tunnel now. Its flanks were heaving with the effort, and blood dripped in a steady stream from its nose, compliments of Alder's sword wound.

The quig was in no hurry now. Its yellow eyes were fixed on Alder, and the spikes on its back scraped the ceiling.

Scrape! Scrape! Scrape!

The only other thing Alder could hear was the sound of his heart.

PENDRAGON
BEFORE THE WAR

BEFORE THE WAR
Book One of the Travelers
Book Two of the Travelers

Coming Soon:

Book Three of the Travelers

PENDRAGON

BEFORE THE WAR

BOOK TWO OF THE TRAVELERS

CREATED BY

D. J. MacHale

WRITTEN BY WALTER SORRELLS

Aladdin Paperbacks
New York   London   Toronto   Sydney

This book is a work of fiction. Any references to historical events, real people, or real locales are used fictitiously. Other names, characters, places, and incidents are the product of the author's imagination, and any resemblance to actual events or locales or persons, living or dead, is entirely coincidental.

ALADDIN PAPERBACKS
An imprint of Simon & Schuster
Children's Publishing Division
1230 Avenue of the Americas, New York, NY 10020
Copyright © 2009 by D. J. MacHale
All rights reserved, including the right of reproduction
in whole or in part in any form.
ALADDIN PAPERBACKS and related logo are registered
trademarks of Simon & Schuster, Inc.
Designed by Mike Rosamilia
The text of this book was set in Apollo MT.
Manufactured in the United States of America
First Aladdin Paperbacks edition February 2009
2 4 6 8 10 9 7 5 3 1
Library of Congress Control Number 2008929799
ISBN-13: 978-1-4169-6523-7
ISBN-10: 1-4169-6523-8

Contents

Aja Killian

ONE

The armored soldiers dragged Aja Killian through the black gates of the castle, down a long, echoing corridor and into a huge—but nearly empty—room. At the far end of the great chamber, a thin, black-clad man stood next to a large wooden throne. The soldiers hauled Aja across the cold marble floor and slammed her to the ground in front of the man.

"Kneel before King Hruth!" shouted one of the guards.

"Avert your eyes, rebel!" shouted the second guard.

As she tried to get her balance, two more guards dragged her friend Nak Adyms into the room. She and Nak had been traveling together in a trading caravan to visit the capital of Qoom. But when they had reached the gates of the castle, a group of soldiers had taken them captive.

Aja looked up at the man by the throne.

"Avert your eyes!" the guard shouted again.

The man—King Hruth, apparently—waved his hand languidly. "It doesn't matter," he said. "You may look upon me if you wish."

King Hruth was a thin man with long black hair and very pale blue eyes. He was dressed entirely in black, with no sign of rank other than a small crest embroidered on his collar. It was the crest of the kingdom of Qoom. He studied Aja for a long time without speaking. Nak knelt next to her, but King Hruth seemed uninterested in him.

"I'm surprised at you, Princess Mara," he said to her finally. "Coming into our city in such a thin disguise! Did you actually think we wouldn't recognize you?"

"I'm a merchant from Rubic City," she said. "My name is Aja Killian. I'm bringing trade goods to sell to the people of your city."

King Hruth laughed genially.

"Tell him, Nak!" she said. "We're merchants."

For the first time King Hruth seemed to acknowledge Nak. "Is it true, Nak?" he said. "Is she really here to sell gimcracks to the people of my realm?"

Nak looked at Aja. Then he stood up and tossed his hair back. He had shaggy brown locks that were always slipping into his eyes. "Of course not," he said. "She's Princess Mara, the rebel leader."

Aja felt her eyes widen. "Hey!" she shouted. "You're supposed to be on *my* side. You said—"

"Maybe you shouldn't have trusted me, huh?" Nak said, smirking.

Aja felt a wave of anger wash through her. Before she could think of an appropriate comeback, a frightening cry cut through the air. It was hard to tell where the sound was coming from. It seemed as though it was welling right up out of the stone floor. Wherever it came from, the howl made the hair stand up on the back of

Aja's neck. It sounded like some kind of wild animal.

"My goodness, the Beast sounds hungry," said King Hruth. "Do you suppose the Beast is hungry, Nak?"

"The Beast is always hungry," Nak said.

King Hruth turned back toward Aja. "There are those who believe that I am not the rightful king of Qoom," he said. "They claim that your little brother, Prince Norvall, should be sitting in this chair instead of me." The king thumped his hand against the throne next to him, then sighed theatrically. "I must tell you, I am growing quite weary of hearing these same tedious arguments. It's time to put them to an end. For good."

The huge iron-bound doors at the rear of the room opened with a loud boom. Aja turned. A large soldier wearing full armor came into the room. In his arms he carried a squirming, howling red-haired boy. Aja guessed him to be eight or nine years old. He looked very familiar.

"Leave him alone!" she shouted.

The king raised one finger. As he did so, there was a loud rasping noise, like two huge pieces of rock being ground against each other.

At the sound, a large rectangular hole began to form in the middle of the great stone floor. The armored soldier carried the squirming boy toward the hole. The grinding noise stopped and the hole ceased growing. The soldier held the boy over the hole.

The boy screamed in terror. "No! No, please! Why are you doing this?"

"Why?" the king said. "Because it pleases me."

With that, the king clapped his hands. The guard let

go of the boy. The boy's mouth opened in a silent scream and his eyes went wide. Then he fell into the blackness.

There was a thump. Then a soft moan.

Then the weird howling cry. "Send some guards into the maze," the king said. "Restrain the boy somewhere down there. Let us see how long it takes the Beast to find him."

"Yes, your majesty!" the soldier said.

Aja turned to Nak and shook her head. "I don't like this, Nak," she said. "I don't like this at all."

Nak laughed. "Hey, *I'm* having fun," he said.

The king turned to one of the other guards, snapped his finger, and pointed at the hole in the floor. "Her too."

The guards grabbed her.

"I've had enough of this game, Nak," she said. "I don't like it."

Nak shrugged.

She held up her left arm, expecting the silver jump-control bracelet to appear so that she could terminate the jump.

But nothing happened.

She held up her arm again, feeling alarmed. Nothing. She had been on literally thousands of Lifelight jumps— and not once had the jump-control bracelet failed to appear when it was time to end the jump. Again she raised her arm.

Still nothing. This was not good!

Two guards seized her arms and started dragging her toward the hole in the floor. Again the bloodcurdling howl rose up out of the floor.

"The maze is a sort of puzzle," King Hruth said, "that I designed sheerly for my own amusement."

Aja managed to briefly yank her hand away from the guard. "Command Level One, password Z-X-E-four-seven-one, invoke jump termination!" she shouted. That was supposed to be the fail-safe command that would end any jump no matter what.

But still nothing happened.

"It might interest you to know," the king said, "that there is an escape route built into the maze. Anyone who finds the route and successfully escapes the maze is automatically granted a royal pardon. No exceptions."

The guards restrained Aja's free arm and pulled her closer to the edge of the rectangular hole in the floor. They stopped only when her toes were sticking out over the edge. She stared down. Below her was a stone shaft leading into inky darkness. Aja's stomach clenched. The guards were holding her so that her weight was out over the darkness. If they let go, she knew she would fall.

"Of course, in all fairness," the king said, "I should mention that no one who has been thrown into the maze has ever escaped."

"Nak!" she shouted angrily. "Nak, the jump won't terminate!"

"My goodness," he said. "How strange."

But the last glimpse she caught of his face—full of fake innocence—told her that he knew more than he was admitting.

One of the guards nudged her gently. And then she was falling down into darkness.

Two

The darkness was endless. There was no up, no down, no cold, no heat—no nothing. Aja waited to hit bottom. But nothing happened. Nothing at all.

And then Aja felt herself waking up. Not the darkness of some frigid old castle, but a warm, pleasant darkness. Despite the warmth though, she was shivering with cold.

She opened her eyes and looked around. She was in her usual jump tube, linked up to the machines that carried her off to the vivid dreams of Lifelight.

She sat up slowly. Something wasn't right, though. She felt puzzled. This wasn't like any Lifelight jump she'd ever been on before. Usually Lifelight jumps were neat and simple. A game, a little scenario, a historical vignette. They were always vivid and engaging. But when you were done, you were done. You climbed a mountain. You water-skied. You jumped out of a flyer. Then you just raised your arm and the silver control bracelet appeared. When you hit the termination button, it was over.

But this one hadn't worked that way. This one had felt less like a jump—and more like a nightmare. And strangely, she still felt cold, the chill of King Hruth's frigid castle still permeating her bones. That had never happened to her on a jump before.

With a flash of anger, she remembered the knowing look on Nak's face as she'd fallen through the floor and down into the hole that led into King Hruth's maze. She slid out of the tube, then pushed open the door of her station. Nak Adyms stood in the doorway next to her cubicle, with his usual smug I-know-something-you-don't grin plastered across his face.

"What did you do?" Aja demanded.

"Keep your voice down," he said. His grin faded, and he looked at her with a cold expression on his face.

"You *tricked* me. You said we were going to do an instructional tandem for history class and—"

He shook his head. "Okay, so I misled you slightly. It's a simulation. A game. A game I designed. But it's all based on real history. King Hruth was a real guy. You can look it up in the history files. He had a maze with a beast in it and everything."

"I don't like games," Aja said. Aja wanted to strangle him. Her hands were trembling. She knew what this was about. She was the top student at the academy. Nak Adyms was number two. And he couldn't stand it. He was always trying to show her that he was smarter than she was. "But that's not why I'm mad. I want to know why my control bracelet didn't work."

Nak cocked his head curiously. "It *what*?"

"Don't play dumb. You heard me back there. I even

invoked termination with a level-one audible command. Nothing happened."

Nak looked blank. "Oh, yeah. I vaguely remember that."

"Oh, please!" Aja said, jabbing her finger at him. "I saw your face."

Nak shook his head. "Hey, I was just amused because you were losing so badly."

"*Losing?* I wasn't losing. I just didn't like being there."

"Come on, Aja, it's a game. Any fool can see that. The point of the game is that you're supposed to go into the maze and rescue the kid. That's how you win the game. Getting captured and all that junk—that's just the introduction to the game."

"Well, there's some kind of *serious* bug in your game. I've never had a control bracelet failure. I've never even heard of one!"

"OE," he said.

"What?"

"OE. Operator error. You must have goofed up. Called out the wrong password or something."

"Nak, don't be ridiculous. I use my password twenty times a day. You think I'd forget it?"

Nak made a face like he didn't care much. "If it wasn't OE, then there's something wrong with Lifelight."

She shook her head. "Jump-control bracelets are hardwired straight to Lifelight's origin code. Everybody has the right to terminate a jump at any time. That's basic jump protocol. You know that. No, Nak, it has to be something you did. Something to do with the way you programmed your game."

Nak's rolled his eyes. "Oh, so now you're saying I hacked the origin code!"

"You know that's totally impossible," Aja snapped.

Nak gave her an enigmatic smile. "Well, then it must have been you, right?"

"Oh?"

"Come on. How many times have I heard you say that simple logic will solve any problem. It's simple logical deduction. If it's not a bug in Lifelight's origin code . . . then it had to be you."

Aja couldn't think of a comeback. He was right. It was hard to dispute his logic.

Nak Adyms turned and walked toward the elevators that ran down the center of the Lifelight pyramid. Aja frowned.

Assembly period started in about ten minutes! As the top student in the class, she was supposed to be there to lead the assembly. Now she was going to be late.

Aja flew into the front door of the academy at precisely 1803 and then charged into the assembly hall, breathing as if she'd just sprinted about a mile. Which she pretty much had. She was surprised to see that assembly period hadn't started yet. Usually everything at the academy ran like clockwork.

She ran down the aisle and up onto the stage, expecting to be scolded unmercifully by Headmistress Nilssin. Oddly, the headmistress just glanced at her and said, "Oh, there you are." Like it was no big deal that she was late.

The headmistress was a tall gray-haired woman with a slight stoop that betrayed her age. She stood up on the podium. "Settle down, settle down!" she said. The kids in the lecture hall quieted slowly.

Normally, Aja made some announcements and then turned the assembly over to Headmistress Nilssin. But today the headmistress skipped over Aja.

"Look, I know you've been hearing rumors," Headmistress Nilssin said. "So let me take a moment to get this settled."

Rumors? What was she talking about?

"A student in the first level has gone missing," the headmistress said.

There was a rustle from the crowd. Kids looked nervously at one another.

"His name is Omni Cader. For those of you who don't know him . . ." She gestured at the holo projector.

A hologram of a young boy with red hair and freckles floated in the air in the middle of the stage. Aja recognized him immediately. He looked just like Prince Norvall—the kid in Nak's game who'd been dumped into the maze.

He'd looked familiar to her during the jump. Now she made the connection: She'd seen him around the academy once or twice. He'd always looked like a sweet kid. Nak must have harvested a scan of him and inserted it as a character in the game.

"Omni is a good boy," the headmistress said. "But for those of you who don't know him, he comes from a somewhat troubled background. He's already run away from the academy a couple of times. But never for this long. Needless to say, we're concerned for his safety. If you would, please keep an eye out for him. If he spoke to anybody, or gave anyone an indication where he might have gone, please contact me or one of your teachers immediately."

Heads nodded throughout the room.

Odd, Aja thought, that the boy had disappeared at the same time as his image had shown up in a Lifelight jump. But she couldn't see any logical connection.

"In the meantime, I'd like everyone who resides in Zetlin Hall to make a top-to-bottom search of the building. I'm going to rely on Aja Killian to organize the search."

Aja saw Nak sitting in the back of the room, slumped down, arms folded. When the headmistress announced that Aja would be leading the search, his eyes narrowed slightly. *Could he possibly be more jealous of me?* Aja thought. As Number One Student, she was entrusted with a lot of responsibilities—most of which, frankly, she could do without!

There were some more announcements, then Headmistress Nilssin said, "That concludes the assembly. Everyone in Zetlin Hall, please stay here." She turned to Aja. "I'll leave it in your capable hands, dear."

Aja stood up and waited until only the students from Zetlin Hall remained. "Okay, people," she said. "Let's keep this short and sweet. Zetlin Hall has four stories and a basement." She pointed at the holo projector. "Holo, please display 3-D map of Zetlin Hall."

Nothing happened.

She repeated herself.

"I'm sorry, I don't recognize your instructions," the voice of the projector said. The projector had an irritatingly condescending voice.

There were a few snickers. She noticed Nak Adyms on

the back row, covering his mouth. She flushed. Something was wrong with the projector apparently.

"Re-initialize holo projector," she said.

"Please enter your password."

She walked to the projector's keypad and typed in her password.

"Password not recognized," the projector said.

There was laughter throughout the room. Aja was angry now. This was twice in one day that something weird had happened with her password. What was going on?

"Well, forget about it," Aja said angrily. "We'll meet in the basement of Zetlin Hall and I'll decide the teams."

"Password not recognized," said a seventh-level kid in the front row, doing a humorous imitation of the projector's irritating voice.

More laughter.

"Ha-ha," Aja snapped.

But that only made things worse. The laughter spread.

They spent most of the afternoon searching Zetlin Hall, the playground, and the surrounding parkland.

They never found Omni Cader. And every time something went wrong, every time some kid got bored or didn't want to do exactly what Aja said, she'd hear it: somebody whispering, "Password not recognized." And then they'd all laugh and laugh and laugh.

THREE

The search consumed most of Aja's afternoon—time she had intended to devote to her senior project. She had been working on a program to reorganize Lifelight's security protocols. Every one of the teachers had told her that if she could pull it off, it would be the most impressive senior project in the entire history of the academy.

It was an audacious project. Because to do it, she would need access to Lifelight's core—the central brain of the Lifelight system. Normally no student at the academy would ever have access to Lifelight's core. The core control room was considered to be a nearly sacred place. At the academy, the Alpha Core was spoken of in whispers. It was where only the best phaders worked—the smartest, the most experienced, the best of the best. It was certainly not the kind of place you let little peons from the academy mess around.

But everybody knew Aja was special. So when she proposed her project and showed just how carefully she'd thought it through, she'd been granted access.

She still had a lot of work in front of her before the project was complete. But first, she had to sort out this stupid password situation.

Aja walked into Lifelight, under the vault of the great pyramid of glass, then down a corridor approaching the large door of the core control room. She paused in the hallway for a moment. She could remember the first time she had come here. It was on a tour of the building with her first-level class. She'd immediately thought, *Someday I'm going to work here!*

It still gave her a thrill to be here.

Several of the senior phaders stood in the corner, laughing about something. Another was sleeping at his terminal, a thin stream of drool slowly descending into his lap. Several sat at their terminals, motionless, bored looking. Another was eating gloid. A big fat pink blob of gloid fell off his spoon onto the terminal controller. The guy didn't seem to notice. Or care.

Back when she first came, she'd been intimidated by them, imagining them to be brilliant, all powerful, all knowing. But these guys? She had to admit they didn't look that intimidating. Actually, they mostly looked bored.

She smiled. Well, maybe some of the phaders were bored here. But not her!

She moved forward, inserted her card key into the slot near the door handle and stepped toward the door.

Which she bumped into, bashing her nose.

"Ow!" she said. Something was wrong with the door. She tried her card again.

Again, nothing.

She realized that whatever had gone wrong with her password had probably affected her access to the control room too. She rapped on the door.

One of the senior phaders, Dal Whitbred, looked up from his terminal at her and waved.

She pointed at the door. Dal frowned, then thumbed a button on the terminal. The door opened.

"Thanks, Dal!" she called as she entered the room. "Something's gone wrong with my password. You think you can help me out?"

"Hey, no problem," he said. Dal was a young guy, kind of cute, with longish brown hair and warm brown eyes. "Just log on with my password and reset yours."

"Um . . ." She looked at him, puzzled. "You're not really supposed to give out your password are you?"

"You going to tell anybody what it is?"

"No," she said.

Dal grinned. "Then we're fine, aren't we?" He scribbled down his password as she sat down at the terminal next to his.

"Thanks." She logged in.

"So it sounds like you're probably gonna get valedictorian, huh?" Dal said.

She looked up from the terminal. "How'd you know that?"

"Oh, your buddy Nak comes in here a lot. He talks about you all the time."

"He *does*?" She'd always thought he hated her.

"Don't tell him *I* said this," Dal said with a grin. "But I think he might have a thing for you."

She laughed harshly. "Not likely! No, he just wants

to beat me. He wants to be Number One Student and take valedictorian."

"Could be," Dal said. "He's a complicated kid." He laughed again. "Between you and me, I think he's got some problems."

"Yeah?"

"Hey, he's a brilliant phader, though. He's been practically living in here lately. I'm surprised you haven't seen him." Dal scratched his head. "No, now that I think about it, he always comes here in the middle of the night. I guess you're probably sleeping when he's in here."

Aja looked at him curiously. "But . . . he doesn't have a job here. He doesn't have clearance. . . ."

Dal smiled. "We kind of adopted him. He's like an informal intern. That kid's a wizard. I've never seen anybody that can make Lifelight jump like he can. Well . . . other than you maybe."

"But—what if he—"

"Hey, believe me, we keep an eye on him to make sure he's not doing anything crazy."

Aja turned back to her terminal. Reconfiguring her password was a simple process. But, still, you had to—

She paused. Strange. It *should* have been a simple process. Now suddenly Lifelight was bringing up menus she'd never seen. For some reason, she couldn't seem to get to the screen she needed in order to change her password.

"What's going on here, Dal?" she said.

Dal rolled his chair over and peered at her screen. "Huh," he said. "Weird." He tapped at the keyboard a few times. "Very weird!" he said. "I've never seen anything like this before."

"What?" Aja said.

"Well . . . it seems as if Lifelight has partitioned your identity. It's put your whole security file behind some kind of firewall."

"But . . ." She stared at the screen. "That's not possible!"

"Scoot over," Dal said. "I need to take a closer look at this."

Something was blinking red on the screen now, a small red flashing icon that she'd never seen before.

"You know what?" Dal said. "I . . . uh . . . I hate to do this to you. But I think this may take a while. Why don't you head back to the academy? I'll call you when I get it sorted out."

"If you don't mind, I'd like to stay and watch."

He cleared his throat. "Um—no, I think—no, I think you need to go home. Right now Lifelight's saying your clearance has been revoked." An alarm began to chime. Everybody in the core control room looked up to see what was going on. Even the drooling guy woke up and looked around.

"Revoked! Why?" Aja felt outraged. Everybody knew she was trustworthy. *Everybody!*

"Seriously. You need to go." All of a sudden Dal was not his usual relaxed self.

"But—"

"Look, there's been a protocol breach here. The Lifelight directors are very strict about this kind of thing."

"Yeah, but—"

"Do you want me to have to call Lifelight Services?"

Aja's eyes widened. Lifelight Services ran the security

force that protected everything connected to Lifelight. "What!"

"Sorry, Aja. You of all people should understand. It's procedure. If Lifelight shuts down an ID . . ." He spread his hands helplessly.

He was right. Security was important. Keeping the core safe was critical. If Lifelight said she needed to go, she needed to go.

Still, it stung.

"I understand," she said softly. She stood and walked to the door. Everyone in the room was looking at her. Her face burned. She knew there had been some talk among them—especially among the old-school senior phaders who felt that letting a kid into the core control room was wrong. Much less letting her fiddle with security protocols.

"I'll be back!" she said forcefully. Then she looked at the locked door, and remembered her useless card.

"Uh . . . can somebody help me get out of here?" she said.

Aja wanted to crawl into a hole and die.

FOUR

The thing she couldn't figure out was, *why had this happened?* Somebody had put up a security firewall around her Lifelight identity. Who? Why? How?

There was no conceivable reason why any of this would happen. Maybe during her work with the security protocols she had triggered some kind of automatic security precaution. She'd never heard of anything like that happening. But maybe it was possible.

No, she didn't want to admit it, but everything pointed in the same direction: Nak Adyms.

The first indication of trouble had been inside his game. First the silver control bracelet malfunction. Then when she invoked termination with an audible, passworded command—still nothing.

But unless Nak had made some kind of very strange mistake in the programming of his game, then it was hard to see any possible answer.

Except one: Nak had hacked the origin code.

Lifelight's origin code—the basic program that ran Lifelight—had been written by the founder of Lifelight, Dr. Zetlin, years and years ago. He had written every line of it. And since then, the origin code had never been touched. Never.

Sometimes phaders joked about hacking the origin code. But it was just a joke. Everybody knew that Dr. Zetlin had installed a maze of security features that made it impossible to—Wait! A maze!

That was it.

Nak's game was a maze. It was a puzzle. It was—

As she walked through the great glass Lifelight pyramid, Aja rapidly thought through the many possible implications of her conclusion. If Nak really had hacked the origin code, then he would have done it for a reason. And what could that reason be?

To show her up, to make her look foolish? No . . . not just that. He was trying to prove that the security innovations she was testing were fundamentally flawed. That's what he was doing. He was trying to wreck her senior project. If he could poke a hole in it, expose it as flawed, her grade for the project would inevitably suffer. In which case—theoretically—he might be able to edge her out for valedictorian.

At that moment a young man with floppy brown hair bounced around the corner. Nak Adyms. "Hey!" he said, grinning. "I was just thinking about you. Did you sort out your little password problem?"

She glared at him. "I think you know the answer to that."

"What!" he said innocently.

"Surely you're aware that any gain in class standing that you might make by crashing my security protocols will be lost when Headmistress Nilssin finds out that you've hacked the origin code."

Nak squinted at her. "I don't know *what* you're talking about."

"Right."

Aja's communicator chimed. She pulled out the small silver device. "Yes?"

"It's Dal," the voice on the other end said. "We've run into a really serious problem. Whatever this program is that's attacked your identity . . . Well, that's only the tip of the iceberg."

"What do you mean?"

"It's starting to move deeper into the core software."

"So you've isolated the program?"

"Well . . . sort of. The program we've located is just a shell. It sits over the top of more programs. But we can see what's underneath it. The shell program is hiding its real function."

"Well, go Command Level One."

"Come on, Aja. We've done that already."

"I wrote a new security facility called—"

"I already tried that. We've tried everything obvious."

"Then why are you calling me?" Aja said.

There was a long pause. "Because the program that crashed your password . . ."

"Yes?"

"Well . . . you wrote it."

Aja felt momentarily confused. "What! That doesn't

make any sense. Why would I write a program that crashed my own identity?"

"Look," Dal said, "I know you've been messing with a lot of Lifelight's deeper code for your project. If you made a little mistake or something, hey, we understand. But you need to tell us."

Aja felt a stab of dread. This was starting to get serious. "I swear!" Aja said. "I didn't do anything. What's the name of this program anyway?"

"It's got some kind of goofy name. Hold on. . . ." She heard some keys clicking. "It's called 'King Hruth's Maze.'"

Her eyes widened. "That's not my program!" she shouted.

"No need to get emotional," Dal said. "Just admit what you did, and we'll figure out how to stop it."

"I didn't do *anything*!"

There was a very long pause. "All right." Dal's voice sounded distant and cold. "If that's the way you want to play it. But I'll be forced to notify the Lifelight directors about what you've done here."

"Dal, how could you even think that—"

"Last chance, Aja. Your little program is already attacking the core."

"No, Dal, I—"

"All right. But don't say we didn't give you a chance."

Her communicator went dead. She started to call Dal back. But what would that do? Right now logic pointed straight at her. If she was going to prove she didn't have anything to do with this problem, she'd have to get more evidence.

Nak was still leaning casually against the wall, a placid smile on his face. "Everything okay?" he said.

"Nak, you framed me!"

Nak shook his head, as if she were speaking a language he didn't understand. "You seem kind of nervous," Nak said. "Maybe a quick jump would calm you down. I have an excellent game in mind that might—"

"This is not funny anymore!" Aja said. "Your clever little program is attacking the core!"

"*My* program? What program? All I'm talking about is playing a game."

Something was forming in her mind. An idea. A plan. She could feel the shape of the idea . . . but she couldn't quite get her fingers around it yet.

"You can't win if you don't play." Nak was still smiling. But she could see something in his eyes underneath the smile—anger, spite, envy.

"The program that's attacking the core—it's *inside* the game, isn't it? You buried it inside a jump program."

Nak laughed. "Boy, you sure are being dramatic."

"You won't get away with this."

"But, just for the sake of argument, if I were going to attack the core using some kind of game program, I wouldn't put it *inside* the game."

She looked at him for a long time. Then it hit her. "It's not inside the game, is it?" she said. Her eyes widened. "It *is* the game!"

Nak raised one eyebrow. "Want to play?"

"Nak," she said, "I just told Dal that I had no idea what King Hruth's Maze was. If I played your game right now, Lifelight would send a message straight to the control room saying I had invoked the program. Dal would think I had just lied to his face. He'd think that I really *was* the one who'd written your nasty little program."

Nak rolled his eyes. "Give me a little credit here. I'll reroute everything so they'll never even know you're jumping. I've got tricks the phaders in the control room can't begin to figure out. Those guys do everything by the book. I can run rings around them. You'd be totally safe."

Aja hesitated. If she was right, the only way to beat the program, to keep it from destroying the core, was to play the game. But if she got caught before she figured out what Nak was up to—well, it could be disastrous. Just for starters, she could kiss valedictorian good-bye. In fact, she'd probably get thrown out of the academy. Even worse, the Lifelight directors could ban her from ever working as a phader. Everything she'd been working for would be down the tubes.

Aja was not a natural risk taker. But right now she didn't see any logical alternative. If she went to Dal and tried to blame everything on Nak, she'd look like a liar. Nak was a good phader. If he'd intentionally made it look as though she had written the program, then talking to Dal right now would only make things worse. The problem was, Nak's program was already munching away at the core. She had to do something to stop it.

But the only way she could think of to stop Nak's program was to jump into his game. Now.

Aja pointed at the tier above her. "Okay, Nak. I see a free jump station up there."

Nak smiled. "I knew you'd see the light eventually."

FIVE

Aja landed with a tooth-jarring thump. Pain shot through her left ankle as the impact smashed her to her knees. She stood, tested the ankle. It hurt a little. But she could tell it wasn't broken or too badly sprained.

She looked around. She lay in a small chamber of closely fitted black stone. Maze? This was no maze. It was a prison cell, barely wide enough for a person to lie down in.

Above her head she saw a bright rectangle of light. Silhouetted in the light was a figure. No, two figures.

One was King Hruth. The other was Nak Adyms.

"Bye-bye!" Nak shouted, waving cheerfully. "Have fun!"

Then the stone above her head began to slide back in place. She could hear the terrible grinding sound again, stone gnashing against stone. Nak's arrogant smile disappeared as the trapdoor closed.

The room was plunged into darkness.

The grinding stopped. Aja felt a terrible sense of

claustrophobia. Her heart raced and her palms were sweating. If she thought it would work, she could activate her silver bracelet and terminate the jump. But like Nak said, he'd hacked all the codes. He'd blocked her. This jump wasn't going to end until Nak felt like ending it. Besides—she was here to solve the puzzle. She couldn't very well quit now.

Aja tried to calm herself, breathing deeply.

Suddenly the grinding noise started again. This time the sound was slightly different and seemed to come from a different place. For a moment she imagined the walls were closing in, preparing to smash her like a bug.

Wait! Light. She could see light—a thin crack, widening slightly at one corner of the room.

The walls were moving! The chamber was opening. As soon as she could, she squeezed out past the still-moving gap between the walls. She found herself in a long stone passage lit by flickering torches lodged in recesses along the wall.

On the walls were carved images. A strange, simian creature recurred in each carving. That must be the Beast that King Hruth had talked about earlier. In each picture the Beast was eating people, tearing them limb from limb, trampling over their bodies.

"Yuk!" Aja said. To think all this nutty stuff came right out of Nak's imagination. You thought you knew somebody and—

The grinding stopped once more. Suddenly the silence seemed extraordinarily intense. She'd never experienced silence like this before. There was literally no sound at all. She could actually hear her own heartbeat, the rush of the blood.

She was breathing very fast, she noticed.

There was a stale, pungent odor in the air. Then she heard something. A loud rustling noise, like a bag of meat being dragged along a floor.

Then a loud, inhuman scream.

The Beast. It was the Beast of the maze. And it was coming for her. She looked behind her. Where before there had been a tiny chamber, now there were three more passages running off in three directions. All three passages seemed more or less identical. Each one had some kind of symbol carved into the rock over the entrance. The passages ran off into the murky distance, until the torch light died out.

She looked over her shoulder. Two yellow eyes appeared around the distant corner at the end of the corridor. A gleam of light on long sharp teeth. The Beast! It was hunched over, walking on two powerful hind legs. Its hair was long and matted. The Beast resembled a monkey, but was much larger and stronger than a person. Its human-looking hands were tipped with long curved talons.

Dread ran through her like a spike between the shoulder blades. She began running, fear driving away all sensation of pain in her ankle. The scream followed her. As she ran down the corridor, other corridors branched off from it. She could hear the thudding of the Beast's feet, growing closer and closer. It was obviously faster than she was.

As big as it was, she could probably turn corners

faster. She turned into another corridor. Then another. Then another. She found herself running past a row of barred cells. Inside the cells were old men, bearded, broken down.

"You'll never make it!" they all shouted. "You're doomed!"

Thanks for the encouragement, she thought. She knew it was all part of Nak's plan to psych her out. But still. It was creepy!

"Doomed!" they moaned. "Doomed!"

She passed the cells and ended up in another corridor. This one was more brightly lit. On the walls, these carvings were bigger, clearer. Above each picture of the Beast was a symbol, some kind of alphabet or pictogram—similar to the ones she'd noticed in the first passageway. It was like nothing she'd ever seen in a history book though. She studied the symbol for a moment, looking for a pattern. Then she realized that now was no time to be messing with puzzles.

She stopped, listened.

Nothing.

No pounding footsteps behind her. No dragging noises. No screaming. She began tiptoeing forward. She must have shaken it!

At the far end, the corridor turned left.

She peered around the corner.

Crouched there, not ten feet away, was the Beast. Its head was lowered, resting its weight on the knuckles of one massive hand, its nose sniffing the ground.

Oh, no! she thought. Somehow she had ended up behind it.

She froze, afraid that even the slightest sound would give her away. Suddenly the Beast stopped sniffing the floor. Its head came up.

Her pulse pounded in her ears. It sounded as loud as a hammer.

The Beast turned, fixed its eyes on her and charged.

There was no escape. *It's all just a Lifelight jump,* she tried to tell herself. *If I can convince myself of that, then Lifelight won't try to shut down my brain when the Beast's jaws clamp down on my—*

Grinding.

Suddenly the grinding noise she'd heard when the walls moved started again.

The Beast froze, looked around. It was no more than five feet from her. But a section of the ceiling was moving downward now. The Beast eyed it nervously, blew several breaths from its large nostrils, and then began backing away.

Apparently, it was not interested in being squashed.

Aja too backed away. Now she could feel the entire floor moving beneath her feet. The grinding sound seemed to invade her bones. It may have saved her life, but it was sure a scary sound. The wall was getting closer and closer, the corridor narrower and narrower.

Suddenly she realized that the threat was no longer the Beast. It was the maze itself! The corridor was squeezing in on her. She sprinted for the far end of the hall.

But as soon as she began to move, she realized she'd never make it. She had figured out a long time ago that she had a sort of computer in her brain that could measure distances, make sense of motion and shapes and sizes, and spit out answers. How close, how far, how many seconds it would take to go from here to there . . .

And the fact was, if the walls kept closing in, she'd never make it.

But she kept running anyway. The terrible claustrophobia was on her again as the walls squeezed tighter and tighter.

As she ran, a voice called to her: "In here!"

She stopped. Where was the voice coming from? The corridor was more than a hundred feet long, without a break.

"Aja! Here!" The voice came from behind her somewhere.

She whipped her head around. Nothing but—Wait! There! As the walls closed in tighter and tighter, she saw that a tiny slit had opened behind her. She hurled herself toward it.

Just in time, she burst through the slit. It was barely large enough to admit a human body. But that was all she needed. She squeezed through, finding herself in a tiny room not much larger than a coffin.

In the dim light, just inches away, she saw a man. He was chained to great rusting bolts driven into the black rock wall.

The only light in the room came from the corridor. As the walls squeezed shut, the light began to die.

Oddly, the chained man was smiling at her.

Then the light was gone. She was trapped! She moaned slightly. This was horrible! This wasn't even a room. It was nothing but a tiny shaft.

"We're gonna die here," she gasped. She tried to tell herself it was all in her mind. It was just a jump, just a fantasy, just a—But her body wanted to explode. She felt herself panting with fear.

"Listen to me," the man said softly. His voice was deep and calm. He sounded like he was on a picnic, not chained to a wall in a stone coffin. "You're okay, Aja. I know you're claustrophobic. But you *will* get out of here."

She tried to calm her panicked breathing. "How do you know who I am?"

"I have come a long way to see you," the man said.

"Who are you? What's your name?"

"My name is Press," the man said. "I've come to tell you something very important."

Then his face began to fade, and the world around her began to disappear.

Six

Hurry! Now!"

"Huh?" Aja felt bleary and strange. It took her a moment to figure out where she was. Back in the Lifelight jump tube. Nak was standing over her.

"We gotta go!" he said in a tense whisper. "Somebody pinged us."

Pinging was a technique that phaders used to contact people inside a jump. If somebody pinged them, it meant that a phader had located them somehow. Busted! This was a disaster. She could get thrown out of the academy. She could—

Nak grabbed her by the hand. "Let's go."

"But . . . if they pinged us, then they know who we are. They know I'm—"

Nak yanked her up off the jump table. He started running. Aja followed him into the hallway. Her legs were stiff and her shoulders hurt. "Run!" he shouted.

She started running too. Though for the life of her she couldn't see why. If a phader had pinged them, then the phader knew who they were. She felt sick with fear. They were going to be in *so much* trouble!

"I rerouted everything," Nak shouted over his shoulder. "Right now they don't know where we are. I changed the registry, too. Our IDs were fake. It was probably just a routine system check. If we can just get out of the building, they'll never know it was us. Run!"

So there was hope. Aja ran faster. Her ankle was hurting though. It was weird. It was almost like the hit her ankle had taken when she fell into the maze had stuck with her after the jump. But that wasn't possible.

They pounded down the softly lit hallways, passing empty jump station after empty jump station. As she ran, she spotted a clock. It was late, almost midnight. Academy students weren't supposed to be at Lifelight any later than eight. She couldn't believe that she'd been playing Nak's game for that long. It seemed like she'd only been in for a few minutes.

Nak shouldered past her. "This way," he said. "Quickly. They'll be back in a couple of minutes."

They retraced their steps, then went through a doorway into an emergency stairwell. She followed Nak into a lower level of the Lifelight pyramid. The lights in the hallway were dim. It was a little creepy.

"What is this place?" Aja said. She thought she had been all over Lifelight. But she'd never been here.

"The old research wing," Nak said. "They used it a lot back when Dr. Zetlin was still perfecting Lifelight. Now it's pretty much deserted. Except for these guys." He pointed into one of the stations. A pair of legs stuck out of the machine that synched you up to Lifelight. "These are hardcore jump phreaks."

She'd heard stories about jump phreaks, people who quit their jobs and just lived in the basements of Lifelight, making unauthorized jumps, sometimes getting so involved in their jumps that they risked starving to death. She'd always figured they were just stories.

Far down the hallway a disheveled man ducked furtively into a booth and slammed the door. An old woman in a strange black dress hobbled toward them. She had something written in tiny letters on a piece of paper that was taped to her clothes. "They're taking your brains!" the old woman shouted. "They're taking your brains!"

"Don't pay any attention to her," Nak said. "She's harmless."

"I don't like this," Aja said.

"Phaders and vedders don't come down here much," Nak said. "We'll be safe. Wait about ten minutes and we can sneak out."

They kept walking down the hallway. From almost every darkened tube, she could see a pair of legs sticking out on the jump table. Every jump at Lifelight was supposed to be attended to by a vedder. Vedders monitored vital signs and made sure no one experienced health problems during a jump. But down here there wasn't a vedder in sight.

She kept looking at the legs sticking out, wondering who these people were. To think that this secret underworld had been here all this time . . . and she'd never known it.

One pair of legs shocked her. It was a kid. Kids

weren't supposed to be in Lifelight past eight o'clock. All she could see was a pair of small green athletic shoes sticking out of the machine.

"Sad, huh?" Nak said, noticing her gaze resting on the green shoes.

"Should we do something about it?"

"Like what?" he said. "Go tell a phader that while we were escaping from an unauthorized jump, we ran across a kid who should be home in bed?"

Aja felt terrible. She knew he was right. But still, it made her feel queasy. This whole situation was so bad! There were no right answers here.

Nak's face softened. "Poor kid. Most likely both his parents are jump phreaks too. If we try to intervene, Lifelight Services will probably grab him. They might even take the kid away from his family. I've seen it happen down here."

"Wow," Aja said.

Nak pointed at the clock. "It's been ten minutes. I think we should be safe. Let's get out of here."

"Okay."

"Our odds are better if we split up," Nak said. "You go that way; I'll go this way."

Aja's heart was racing as she walked out one of the service exits of the Lifelight pyramid. Nobody seemed to pay any attention to her. But that didn't stop the sick feeling in the pit of her stomach.

She turned the corner and started walking down the broad avenue that led back toward the academy. The streets were dark and empty.

As she approached the building, she saw two figures standing near the entrance to her dormitory. One of them was Nak. The other was tall and thin. A teacher from the academy?

Aja wasn't sure. She didn't want to be seen out this late, so she ducked behind a bush. Nak and the other man talked for a moment. Then they separated, and Nak disappeared through the front door of Zetlin Hall.

The man stood for a moment watching him go. His face was shadowed in darkness. Aja wasn't sure what it was about him, but something made her feel frightened.

Suddenly the man turned. A beam of light from the streetlamp overhead illuminated his face momentarily. Aja gasped.

The man turned and melted back into the darkness.

She had only gotten the briefest glimpse of the face. But there was no mistaking those pale blue eyes. She'd recognize them anywhere. It was King Hruth.

SEVEN

The next morning Aja awoke to the sound of pounding on her door. She opened it and looked out.

Headmistress Nilssin stood in the hallway. Behind her was a large, burly man with a shaved head. He wore the insignia of Lifelight Services on his shoulders. A visit from Lifelight Services was never a good thing.

Aja's heart raced.

"Hi, Headmistress," Aja said, trying her best to sound confident and unconcerned. "Something wrong?"

Headmistress Nilssin's face was tense, and there were spots of color high on her cheeks. "This man is from Lifelight Services. I'll let him speak for himself."

"Aja Killian?" the man said.

"Obviously," Aja snapped.

"Aja Killian," the burly man said, "on behalf of the directors of Lifelight, this constitutes formal notification of the suspension of your Lifelight identity and privileges. Certain irregularities have been flagged on your profile. Until further notice, you will not be permitted to enter the Lifelight premises or to utilize Lifelight equipment. Pending resolution of those irregularities—"

"Irregularities!" Aja shouted. "Somebody is hacking into the core. And it's not me. I happen to know—"

Headmistress Nilssin held up her hand. "Aja, stop talking. Now! Not another word. You have rights. Anything you say at this point could be misconstrued or used against you. Just . . . be quiet. I'm handling this."

"Headmistress Nilssin," the older man said, "if the young lady is willing to cooperate, we might be willing to consider leniency. Perhaps only a five-year suspension of her privileges could be arranged if she—"

Five years! Aja felt like a giant steel clamp had been tightened around her chest.

"Sir," Headmistress Nilssin interrupted, "you have made your notification. I would request that you leave the academy now."

"I'm in the middle of a major project at Lifelight!" Aja said. "I have to—"

"Aja!" Headmistress Nilssin said. "Quiet."

The man from Lifelight Services glanced at Aja as if she were a bug he was about to squash. Then he turned back to Headmistress Nilssin. "I will be forced to notify the directors of your lack of cooperation."

"I am simply insisting that you respect the legal rights of my student. You have done your job. Thank you. Now go."

The man's eyes narrowed slightly. Then he turned on his heel and marched away.

After he was gone, Headmistress Nilssin turned to Aja and said, "Look, Aja, I don't know what's going on. I don't know what you're involved in—"

"It's not me!" Aja said. "I'm being framed!"

"Aja, listen to me. Listen carefully. Dal Whitbred has showed me the evidence against you. It's very, very strong. But right now they're too busy trying to stop this program from destroying the core to worry about you personally. Lifelight could be severely damaged within a matter of hours. In fact, things are so desperate that they've asked me to lend my expertise." As Aja knew, Headmistress Nilssin had once been one of Dr. Zetlin's top assistants during the early days of Lifelight. She was still a top authority on the inner workings of the system. "On top of that, we still haven't found Omni Cader. Right now I just don't have time to discuss the matter with you."

"But—" She wanted to explain about Nak's game.

Headmistress Nilssin raised her hand sharply. "Go to class. Follow your normal routine. And needless to say, don't even *think* about trying to go over to the Lifelight pyramid."

"Headmistress Nilssin, look—"

"We'll talk later." Headmistress Nilssin walked swiftly away.

Aja went back in her room and gently closed the door. She felt as if she'd been punched in the stomach. The fact that the Lifelight directors had personally acted to suspend her privileges—well, there were just no words to express how sick she felt. What was wrong with these people? It wasn't fair. Why didn't they believe her? She was arguably the best student the academy had ever had. Not *once* had she ever broken a rule, ever cheated on an exam, or ever been a behavior problem. Not once!

Her mind began clicking through the alternatives. Nak *was* smart. There was no doubt about that. Smarter than she'd given him credit for. If he had done things right, it might literally be impossible for her to prove she had nothing to do with the program.

In which case, she only had one alternative: finish the game. And win it!

She picked up her communicator, called Nak. "It's me," she said. "Lifelight Services has suspended my privileges. Can you get me into Lifelight?"

Nak started laughing. "I was wondering when you'd call."

Within minutes they were inside the huge Lifelight pyramid, heading down into the old research wing. Nak had all kinds of tricks up his sleeve—fake ID chips, bogus passwords, and an apparently encyclopedic knowledge of the architecture of the building. As they were walking down the hallway, she noticed a pair of green shoes still sticking out of the same jump tube.

"That kid's still here," she said. "I wonder who he is."

She started to poke her head into the station to look into the tube at the boy's face.

Nak grabbed her arm. "You want to play the game or not?" he said sharply.

"Okay, okay," she said.

"Here," Nak said. "Your tube's ready. This time there's no way they'll find you. I took extra precautions."

She looked him in the eye. "You sure?"

He nodded.

She walked in and lay down on the jump table.

"Go save Prince Norvall, Aja," Nak said as he leaned over her to plug in the neural connection wires. Then he smiled coldly. "If you can . . ."

EiGHT

She entered the jump in the tight rock shaft again, the cold walls pressing against her. It was completely dark. Aja felt her skin crawl. Even though she knew it was just a jump, she still felt claustrophobic.

As she tried to calm herself down, she could hear breathing across from her. She'd forgotten all about that. She'd been trapped in here with a man. A man who'd said his name was Press.

"Ah," the man named Press said. "There you are. We had a bit of an interruption."

"I wouldn't have thought you'd notice," she said.

"I'm not part of Nak's game," the man said. "I'm like you. I tandemed into his jump. The difference is, Nak doesn't know I'm here."

"What?" Aja said. "How's that possible?"

"That's not important," the man named Press said. "We don't have much time. So listen carefully."

"Okay." She cleared her throat. The sound was flat and compressed inside the rock tomb. She tried to breathe slowly. But her skin was clammy, and she felt a little light-headed. "So why are you in Nak's game?"

"I came to tell you about your destiny."

Okay, this was getting more strange and improbable by the moment. "My *destiny*?"

What was he getting at? She tried to focus on what he was saying, tried to push aside the fact that she was entombed in a coffin-size slab of rock.

"You and I are what's known as Travelers," the man named Press said. "We are engaged in a great battle against forces that seek to destroy Veelox. But not just Veelox. There are other worlds similar to Veelox. Their fate hangs in the balance."

"Okay, okay, hold on," Aja said. "You said you're not part of Nak's game."

"Correct."

"So this stuff you're telling me—"

"Also has nothing to do with Nak's game. Nothing *directly*."

"Then, uh . . . why not just come talk to me at the academy or something?"

"Saint Dane is very powerful on Veelox. The academy is part of his strategy here. He's watching it very closely."

"Saint *Who*?"

"I'm sorry. Saint Dane is the adversary of the Travelers. You'll know him as a tall thin man with long black hair."

"That sounds like King Hruth."

"For the purposes of Nak's game, yes. In real life he's taken the identity of the man you saw talking to Nak the other day, a man name Allik Worthintin. He's a director of Lifelight."

"But . . . how . . ."

"We don't have much time. Save your questions. All I can tell you is that you'll soon be ready to assume your responsibilities as a Traveler. Other Travelers may come to visit you. When they do, protect them from Saint Dane."

Something in the back of Aja's mind said, *This whole thing is totally ridiculous. And, despite what Press is saying, he's probably just another trick in Nak's nasty little game.* But the good thing was that his calm voice was keeping her claustrophobia at bay.

"Now, it's time for you to go."

"But, I need more answers to—"

"We're in a shaft. If you climb up my chains, you'll find a ladder cut into the rock. Climb up to the top of the shaft. When you get there—"

"But what about you?"

"As long as you win the game, I'll be fine. My jump will terminate, and I'll flume off to some other territory, happy as a clam."

Flume? What was he talking about? What was a flume?

"Well, what if I *don't* win? What if the Beast catches me?"

"Don't think about that."

There was a brief silence. Aja was putting things together, little slivers of evidence that had been assembling and reassembling in her head.

"I noticed something strange the last time I finished my jump," she said. "It was cold in King Hruth's castle. After I finished the jump, I kept shivering. That's not supposed to happen."

"As you know, Aja, there is an intimate neural connection between your brain and your body. Lifelight taps into that connection. As far as your brain knows, Lifelight *is* reality. Back when Dr. Zetlin designed Lifelight, one of the biggest hurdles he had to get over was the feedback loop between the body and the mind. If somebody tripped and fell in Lifelight, their leg would hurt when they finished the jump."

"That happened to me this morning!" Aja said. "I hurt my ankle in the jump. When I got out, I was limping."

"Sure. But it can be a lot worse. Back when Dr. Zetlin was first testing Lifelight, several people actually died. There was some debate about the cause. But it was suspected that it had something to do with the neural feedback loop. So he tested it himself. He went on a jump in which he crashed a vehicle into a wall. He almost died. His heart stopped, and he spent a week in the hospital."

"Okay, but they solved all those problems," Aja said. "There's a damping program in the origin code that cuts the neural feedback loop when anything happens that would hurt your body. Lifelight's a hundred percent safe."

"Unless . . ."

Aja gasped. "Are you saying that Nak interfered with the neural damping protocols?"

Press didn't answer.

"Oh my god!" she said. "But—"

"Right now all the modifications he's made to the origin code only apply inside his game. But if the program succeeds in taking over the core . . ."

Aja felt her eyes widen. "You're saying——"

"That's right. Every single jumper in a Lifelight pyramid would be at risk."

"But . . . that's like half the people in Rubic City!"

Press said nothing.

Once again, Aja was aware of the walls around her, the oppressive silence, the darkness. She shivered.

And then something else struck her. The pair of green sport shoes sticking out of the jump tube. The bare legs of the boy in the tube had been freckled. Like a red-haired boy's would be. And when they'd shown the hologram of Omni Cader during assembly, he'd been wearing red shoes. She hadn't made the connection until just now.

"Prince Norvall," she said. "The point of the game is to save Prince Norvall. I thought that Nak had just harvested his image. But he didn't, did he?"

"No," Press said.

"Omni Cader's in this jump too, isn't he? He's trapped in the game."

"That's right. And if you don't save him, he'll be its first casualty."

For a moment, dread sluiced through her. But then she took a deep breath. She wouldn't let Nak get away with this. "I'll figure it out," she said firmly. "Nak can't beat me. I'm smarter than he is."

"True." She sensed that Press was smiling at her. "Of course, that doesn't mean you'll beat him."

Aja's breathing quickened. "This game is a puzzle. Nak told me there's a way out. He's too vain to have lied to me about that. There has to be a solution. A clear, logical solution."

Press didn't say anything. But she got the impression he was laughing silently.

"What!" she said angrily.

Before he could answer, the grinding noise began again. She felt the vibration running through the rock.

"What are you laughing about?" she said. "This isn't funny."

"Sometimes the solution to a problem is that there *is no solution*," he said.

"That doesn't make sense!" Aja said. "Every problem has a logical solution."

"Now's not the time for philosophical debate," Press said. "Go!"

The grinding was getting louder. She could feel the vibration through the rock. She felt in front of her until her fingers closed around the chain.

"Just step on me," Press said. He must have felt her hesitate, because he added, "Don't worry about me. I've been through lots worse stuff than being walked on." Then he laughed loudly. There was something reassuring about him, something that made her feel safe.

She put one foot on the chain around his wrist. Press grunted. It was obviously a little painful. But then she felt him lifting her into the air. She slid her hands up the shaft until she found a slot like the bottom rung of a ladder. She hauled herself up and began climbing.

"Remember." Press's voice echoed up toward her. "You are a Traveler. You're destined for this."

She kept climbing until she felt her head bang against the ceiling.

"Ow!" she said.

Then the grinding stopped. She felt behind her. The shaft had disappeared. She was in another room. From the way sound echoed in the chamber, she was sure it was quite large.

It was also pitch black. She began feeling her way along the hard stone, moving farther into the large room. As she moved, she felt objects on the floor. Some were hard and metallic. And some were rounded and softer. Wood, maybe.

They clattered as she moved over them.

And then she realized, as her fingers brushed over a large round object with several holes in it . . . No, not wood.

Bone. It was a skull.

She was crawling over bones. Bones and armor and shields.

Her blood ran cold for a moment. She paused. What *was* this place? And then she heard it. Somewhere in the distance, a soft snuffling sound. Then a dragging sound, like a bag full of rocks being hauled across a floor.

The Beast. Somewhere out in the darkness was the Beast.

How far away was it?

Close enough. Close enough that it would find her. Maybe if she crawled back down the shaft. She felt the wall behind her. The shaft was gone! The wall was completely smooth—other than a row of small holes.

What could she do? How could she get away if she couldn't even see? She felt blindly around her. Maybe there was another passage somewhere!

Her hands closed around something. A thigh bone?

Wait . . . no. It was the handle of an old spear. She felt her way up to the top until she reached the point. It was still sharp. A spear!

The snuffling stopped. Then the Beast screamed once. It knew she was there, Aja was sure of it.

Suddenly she had a thought.

"Hey!" she shouted. "Come on! Come and get me!"

There was a brief moment of silence. Then she heard it. The Beast was coming for her, charging through the dark. Aja felt behind her. The holes! Where were they?

Finally she found one. It was chest high. She thrust the hilt of the spear into it so it stuck straight out from the wall.

Footsteps thudded toward her. How far away was the charging Beast now? She couldn't tell. Close. Very close.

"Come on!" she shouted. "Come get me!"

Closer. Closer.

Just as she felt that the Beast was on her, she dove to her right.

As she smashed painfully into the unforgiving rock floor, she heard a massive impact. The Beast had hit the wall. And if her plan had worked, it had impaled itself on the spear.

On cue the Beast screamed. This time it was not a scream of anger. It was a scream of pain.

Perfect! She'd skewered the Beast. Or, more accurately, it had skewered itself. The question was, how badly. Aja decided there was no point in sitting around waiting to find out. She started running as fast as she could. She figured if she slammed into something or tripped over something— hey, that was better than getting eaten by the Beast.

Behind her she heard the Beast thrashing wildly.

The Beast screamed again. She tripped, righted herself, tripped again, then continued on. And as she did, she heard footsteps. The Beast was following her. It was hurt. But by no means was it dead.

She ran as fast as she dared.

But the Beast ran faster. She could hear it, getting closer and closer.

I'm not gonna make it! Aja thought.

She literally felt its breath on her neck.

Oh, well, she thought.

And then suddenly she was airborne, falling through some kind of hole, out into space.

She hit the hard ground with a painful thud. She somersaulted to her feet. *What now?* she thought.

The answer came before she had a chance to decide for herself. The great horrible grinding noise had begun again. And as it did, light flooded into the chamber. She could still see up into the chamber above. The dying Beast was thrashing and rolling in pain. It stopped moving just as the door to the upper chamber slammed shut.

Yes! I've done it! I've killed the Beast. For a moment she felt triumphant. But then she realized that killing the Beast was only the first step in winning the game. She still had to find Omni Cader . . . and then escape the maze.

A light shone from a hole in the ceiling, beaming directly on a symbol carved into the wall. There had been symbols like this in every chamber. They looked like mathematical symbols, but they weren't any kind of symbol she recognized.

Mathematical symbols. Something was tugging at the

back of her mind. Mathematical symbols. Why was she thinking about mathematical symbols when—

Again, the grinding noise. Again, the walls began to move . . . revealing a passage much like the first one she had entered when she was thrown down here. She began running down the passage. Now that the Beast was no longer a threat, she didn't care how much noise she made.

"Omni!" she called. "Omni, where are you?"

For what seemed like hours, she ran through the ever-shifting maze, calling and calling. Just when she had despaired of finding the boy, she heard a high, thin voice.

"Hey! Over here!"

Where "over here" was, Aja wasn't quite sure. She blundered through the maze. And then the walls moved again.

And then . . . there he was. Not fifty feet away from her.

Omni Cader sat in a heap, pale face smudged with dirt, his red hair a mess. He looked scared out of his mind. A single thin chain of gleaming steel led from his ankle to an iron stud driven into the wall. "Aja? Is that you? Aja Killian?"

She nodded.

"What's happened to me?" he shouted. "I can't get out of Nak's jump. My bracelet isn't working!" He held up his arm.

"Don't worry!" she shouted back. "I'm getting you out."

She ran toward him.

"No!" the boy screamed. "Not yet!"

Aja halted about twenty feet from the boy. He was in a small chamber just tall enough to lie down in. The door was open . . . but Omni didn't come out.

"What's wrong?" Aja said.

"The door shuts really fast. If you don't time it right, it'll—"

Before he could finish his sentence, the door to the chamber slammed down. It was a massive slab of rock. If she'd been standing there, it would have squashed her like a bug.

In the center of the rock was a large symbol, similar to the others she'd seen in the maze.

After a moment the entire passage began to move, squeezing shut. She dove backward until she reached another passage. Soon the passage to Omni's cell was gone completely.

What was she going to do? She looked around. Symbols on the walls again. What was it about—

Suddenly it hit her. Math! That was the trick. The maze was a mathematical puzzle. Lifelight was a computer. Computers ran on math. There were symbols on all the walls of the maze. But there was some kind of pattern to the way the walls moved here. Math was just patterns. Right? Maybe they weren't mathematical symbols she'd learned in school. But that didn't mean they weren't part of a mathematical sequence. If she could figure out the pattern that controlled the walls, she could figure out how to get out of the maze.

On some level, the mathematical structure of the maze had to be connected to the structure of the program that

Nak had sent to take over the core. By solving the puzzle, that is, by getting Omni Cader out of the maze—she'd shut down the program. And in so doing, she'd save the core. Along with the lives of hundreds—probably even thousands—of people.

For a moment the enormity of the task in front of her made her feel sick to her stomach.

Focus, Aja! she thought. *It's just math! You know how to do this.*

She waited until the grinding began. The walls began moving, the entire maze reconfiguring again. The grinding stopped. She kept count in her head of the seconds as they passed. Then she just sat down on the floor and waited, letting three more cycles pass.

Yes! It was regular as clockwork! The walls moved for exactly thirty seconds. And they moved on one-minute intervals. Not every single minute. But each move began anywhere from one to five minutes after the previous one. Exact to the second.

She began scribbling on the floor with her finger, making patterns in the grime that coated the rock. The symbols on the walls were suddenly as clear in her head as—

And then she had it! The pattern. The walls changed at regular intervals. And the symbols on the walls corresponded to . . . well, she wasn't sure what. Not quite yet. It had something to do with the pattern of the passages. The maze was made of rock. Even if that rock was just a pattern in the Lifelight computer, still, it was modeled on real rock. It had to act like real rock. It couldn't melt and reform. It couldn't pass through other rock. So there had to be a limited number of configurations to the maze.

And one of those configurations had to lead out of the maze. If it didn't, then Nak's game was unwinnable.

Whatever you might say about Nak, she was pretty sure he wasn't a cheater. Not by his own definition anyway. He wanted to prove he was smarter than she was. Which meant he'd want to beat her fair and square. There *had* to be a pattern and there *had* to be a way out.

The grinding began again. Again she had to flee to avoid getting squashed.

When the grinding finally stopped, it hit her. There were five symbols, five configurations of the maze. They were running in a sequence. But the sequence was changing. It was a complex numerical puzzle. She just had to figure out the sequence.

As soon as the walls stopped moving, she began scrawling on the grimy floor again.

There! She had it! The sequence ran backward. Eventually it would hit a stopping point.

What then? Zero. The final configuration was zero: no symbols.

The grinding began again. "Help! Aja, help!"

Again she had come to the end of the short passage leading to Omni's cell. There was something different about the cell this time though, she realized.

"It's getting smaller!" Omni shouted. "You have to do something!"

"Wait, Omni!" she called. "I'm gonna get you out. But I have to figure out how to—"

The huge door slammed shut.

Wait. She stared. On the door was a sixth symbol. That couldn't be right. The sequence only had five symbols.

Then she realized she'd been wrong this whole time. There weren't five possible configurations. There were six. When the sequence of numbers ended, the sixth configuration would happen. And that would end it all. Something terrible would happen to Omni. Probably the walls of his cell would move together and . . .

And that would be the end of Nak's game.

She scribbled furiously on the floor. To her horror she realized that the sequence had almost run its course. There were five more reconfigurations. Then the game was over. Five moves to go.

From above her head, she heard laughter. She looked up and saw a tiny hole in the ceiling. An eye looked down at her.

She heard Nak's mocking voice. "Took you long enough," he said, laughing some more.

"The final configuration," she called back. "It squashes the place where Omni's chained up. But it also opens the maze, doesn't it?"

"You still have time to get out," Nak called. "I don't think you can get Omni out too, though. Save yourself or save him. I don't think you can save both him and yourself in five moves."

She continued scribbling. Then she saw it. Yes! There was a solution. Nak was wrong. She *could* do it in five moves. Three moves to get to Omni, two moves to get out.

Nak continued to taunt her as she scribbled the

symbols on her arm. Then she leaned over and erased her calculations from the floor with her hand. She had to follow the sequence of symbols each time. If she did it right, the symbols would lead her to Omni again.

The grinding began. Move five. She scanned the walls for symbols. There! She ran down the passage, looking for the next symbol in the sequence. There! She turned. One more and—

The grinding began again. Wait! She spotted the final symbol in the sequence just in time to make her way into the next chamber before the door slid shut. She waited breathlessly.

As soon as the next reconfiguration began, she was off and running. This time it was easier. She knew exactly what she was looking for. Again she found herself standing at the door covering the passage that led to Omni.

Two minutes later the grinding began again. Move three. She waited until she saw Omni.

"Come out!" she shouted.

"I can't," Omni screamed. He pointed to the door. "It'll drop on me."

"No!" she shouted back. "There's a way. Come out all the way. The door will drop on the chain and break it. Then we'll run."

Omni shook his head. "I thought of that already. The chain's too short."

"Maybe it *was*. But it's not now. See?" She pointed at the back wall where the steel chain was attached. "The wall moved."

"But—"

Without another thought, she charged into the room

and dragged the boy out. He struggled furiously. "No!" she shouted. "You have to come out all the—"

Wham!

The giant stone door dropped.

Omni screamed. In horror, Aja looked to see if she'd been wrong. Had the door dropped on his leg?

No. He'd gotten out completely. But the steel chain was so close that it had just torqued his ankle a little. More important, though, the chain had been broken by the weight of the falling door.

"Let's go!" she shouted. The walls of the short passage were grinding shut.

"I can't," Omni whispered. "My ankle. I think it's broken."

She grabbed the boy in her arms and ran. The walls were closing in and in and in and . . .

Then they were into the next chamber.

The grinding stopped. Three moves down, two to go.

"Why can't I get out of the game?" Omni said. Tears were running down his face now. "I don't understand! Nak said it would be fun!"

"It's gonna be okay," Aja said softly, stroking the boy's hair. "I'm gonna get you out of here."

She sat, cradling the crying boy and saving up her strength. She hadn't calculated on having to carry the kid. She just hoped she had the strength to make the next two moves in time. She stared at the symbols on her arm, memorizing the sequence. The key would be spotting them quickly and then—

The grinding started.

She leaped to her feet, threw Omni over her shoulder

like a bag of laundry, and then sprinted down the next hallway. Then left. Then right. Omni moaned softly as she staggered through the maze.

And then she reached the final chamber. "One more move," she whispered, setting Omni on the floor. Her breath was heaving and her lungs were burning. By herself the maze wouldn't have been too hard to get through. But carrying the boy? It was brutal.

Before she could catch her breath, the grinding began.

Final move! She picked Omni up and began to run, moving through the final sequence. Left. Down a shaft. Up a flight of stairs. One final symbol. Where was it? Where was it?

There!

She dashed down the final passage. She'd only made it about halfway before the grinding began again. This time it was the ceiling coming down. She wasn't sure she'd make it. Her arms were sore from carrying Omni, and her lungs felt as if they were full of burning needles.

Just a little farther! The ceiling was so low now that she had to run in a crouch. Just a little farther. She could see the final chamber now. Light—natural light!—was flooding through it. Faster! Faster!

But she still had a little farther to go. And her head was scraping the ceiling. She dropped to her knees, yanking Omni behind her.

Omni howled. "It's gonna squash us! It's gonna—"

And then they were free!

Cold air flooded the room. In front of them was a huge open gate. Beyond that was the great frozen lake that lay on the eastern side of Qoom. Free! They were free!

She set Omni down and raised her fists.

"We did it!"

Omni blinked. "We're free? We're out? The game's over?"

Aja grinned. "The game's over," she gasped. "All we have to do is walk out."

Omni whooped. They began walking slowly toward the gate.

And then, with a massive, horrible thud, a great wall of rock thundered down and slammed into the floor, cutting off the gate and plunging them into darkness.

Aja's heart went into her throat. What had just happened? She'd solved the puzzle! And now Nak had somehow snatched it away. But how? She'd beaten the game!

For the first time in hours she became aware of her physical surroundings again. She had forgotten how frigid it was in the maze, the oozing rock walls making the maze cold as a refrigerator.

"What are we gonna do?" came Omni Cader's high, thin voice.

"I don't know, Omni," she said. "I really don't know."

NINE

Shivering. Aja's first sensation as she resurfaced from the jump was *cold*. Everything was cold. She lay in the jump tube for a long time, hugging herself and shivering uncontrollably. Her arms and legs were sore, as if she'd been punched repeatedly.

But that wasn't the worst thing.

Failure. Total failure. A cloud of misery hung over her. She had failed to beat Nak's game.

"Is she out?" a voice said. "Is she out now?"

"I think so," another voice said. "But she's in bad shape. I've never seen anything quite like this before."

A jolt of panic ran through Aja. *Oh, no!* Somebody had found her. Before she had a chance to move—or even think—two strong arms slid her out of the jump tube. Around her was a half circle of faces. Headmistress Nilssin. The man from Lifelight Services who'd come to her room this morning. Dal Whitbred. A senior vedder, working furiously at the controls of the health unit. And a tall thin man with long black hair and pale blue eyes.

What was it the man in the maze had said his name was? Allik? Yes, Allik Worthintin.

Headmistress Nilssin was shaking her head. "I can't believe it," she said. "I can't even tell you how disappointed I am in you."

Aja was still shivering so hard she could barely sit up.

"Stand up," Allik Worthintin said.

"I still need time with her," the senior vedder said. "She's still not stable."

"I don't care," Allik Worthintin said. "Stand up, young woman."

Aja stood unsteadily.

"Do you have any concept of the problems your little stunt is causing?" Allik Worthintin said. "Your program has taken over eleven percent of the core."

"Twelve," said Dal Whitbred.

"Whatever," the Lifelight director said.

"Sir, I have to protest," the vedder said, still hunched over his health unit. "Her vital signs are—"

Allik Worthintin ignored him. "You're coming with me, Aja," he said. "You're going to sit down in my office, and you're going to tell us exactly and precisely how to shut down your little program."

"It's not *mine!*" Aja said. "How many times do I have to tell you. It's . . ."

And then something terrible occurred to her. She'd seen Allik Worthintin with Nak. Why would somebody as important as a Lifelight director be hanging around with a sixteen-year-old kid? It didn't make sense. Unless . . .

Unless Allik Worthintin knew exactly what Nak was up to already. The man in the maze, Press—he had said that Allik Worthintin was really Saint Whatever-his-name-was.

Aja's teeth started chattering.

"Look at her, sir!" the vedder said. "Her lips are blue!"

"Look," Aja said. "I'm trying to *stop* the program. It's a game."

"Young lady," Headmistress Nilssin said, "if you think this is a game—"

"No! Not that kind of game. The program that's attacking the core—it's a game. It's a tandem jump. And Omni Cader is still inside the jump. We have to get him out!"

Headmistress Nilssin looked at Dal Whitbred.

"Come on!" Aja said. "Follow me. I'll show you. If you managed to get me out of the game, you can get him out too. He'll verify everything I'm saying."

"Secure her," Allik Worthintin said to the burly man from Lifelight Services.

But before he could move, Headmistress Nilssin stepped in front of him. "That boy has been missing for two days," she said. "If there's even a chance Omni's here, we need to know now." Then she turned to Aja. "Show us."

"He's just down the hall," Aja said. She stepped past the burly man as quickly as her wobbly legs would allow. She was feeling terrible, shivering as if she had a fever. And her entire body felt bruised from her encounter with the Beast. She walked down the hall to the tube where she'd seen the green shoes.

Empty.

The tube was empty.

"But—"

"Is this it?" Headmistress Nilssin said.

"Yes," Aja whispered. The tubes were numbered. And Aja never forgot a number. This was the right one. Only . . . Omni Cader wasn't in it anymore.

Aja put her face in her hands. Somehow Nak must have known they were coming. He must have moved Omni to another tube. For a moment she felt like just lying down on the floor and bawling.

Dal Whitbred was whispering into his communicator. After a moment he put it back on his belt. "Director Worthintin," he said, "it's up to thirteen percent. The program seems to be accelerating."

"Get her upstairs," Allik Worthintin said. "Five minutes alone with her and I'll get to the bottom of this!"

Suddenly Aja's mind flashed back to the maze. That man inside the maze, Press, had told her that she was special. He had said she was a Traveler, that it was her destiny to fight for Veelox. His calm voice came back to her. *Sometimes the solution is that there is no solution.* What did he mean by that?

She turned to Dal Whitbred, grabbed his arm. "Dal, please!" she said. "I think I can stop it. Just give me one more chance!"

Allik Worthintin snapped his fingers at the burly Lifelight Services man. "Now. Take her."

"Please, Dal!" She tightened her grip on his arm. "I swear I was only trying to stop this thing. I *have* to jump if I'm going to stop the program."

Dal Whitbred studied her face. It was obvious he wanted to believe her.

"It's *me*, Dal! Have I ever given you any indication that I would try to mess up Lifelight? Headmistress Nilssin? Come on! That's not me."

Dal and Headmistress Nilssin looked at each other.

"Nothing else is working," Dal said.

Headmistress Nilssin gave him a slight nod.

"Absolutely not," Allik Worthintin said. "I'm going to question her personally. And I'm going to do it now." He pointed his finger at Dal Whitbred. "That's an order!"

Dal Whitbred swallowed. "Do you have the full authority of all the directors, sir?" he said. "Because unless you have the full vote of the directors on this matter, I have operational authority to do what I think is right. And I think we're out of options here."

Allik Worthintin's blue eyes bored into Dal's face. "Are you willing to stake your job on it?"

"Yes, sir, I am." Dal's voice was firm and calm.

Allik Worthintin said nothing.

As the two men locked eyes, the senior vedder hustled up behind them. He was a roly-poly man with a nervous face. "Something has gone wrong with the neural buffering," he said. "I can't guarantee her safety."

"I don't care," Aja said. "I'll take the chance."

Finally Director Worthintin threw up his hands, his lips curling in anger. "All right. Fine. I wash my hands of this." He turned and stalked away.

"Get me back in," Aja said.

TEN

Cheater!" Aja shouted into the darkness. "You're a cheater! You're not smarter than I am! You're not better than I am! You're just a worthless little cheater!"

For a moment there was no sound. Just an empty, cold, featureless darkness. Omni Cader sniffled once.

Then, above them, a small square of light appeared. An eye looked down. "Oh, you're so predictable." Nak's voice came out of the little hole.

"Predictable?"

Aja felt a horrible sick sensation in her stomach. What if she had been wrong about Nak? What if Nak was never going to let her out of here? There would be more Beasts. More sequences. More tricks. More gimmicks.

"I'm not a cheater," Nak said. "I'm just smarter."

"No offense, Nak," she said, "but I've been better in math than you from day one."

"Exactly!" Nak said. There was a note of triumph in his voice.

The tiny door through which Nak was looking slid shut. The room went dark again.

And then it hit her. She hadn't looked deeply enough into the problem. There was a sequence to the rooms, yes. But there was also a sequence to the timing, too. The gaps between reconfigurations ranged from one to five minutes. There was probably some kind of sequence there too. And if there was a relationship between the time and the symbols . . . well, it would get into some *seriously* complicated math.

After a while the grinding noise began again. *A new sequence,* she thought. A new sequence would be beginning.

But how did it start? Was it random?

"What do we do now?" Omni said.

"I don't know," Aja said. "I have to do some calculations. Let's move to a room with better light."

"But . . . I thought you said you'd get us out," Omni said.

"I will," she said. But she wasn't feeling all that confident.

A door began to open.

"Let's go," she said. She put her arm under Omni's shoulder, supporting him. They walked slowly into the next chamber. And stopped.

After a while the grinding ceased.

"What's in here?" Omni said. "Why don't we keep moving?"

She shook her head. "I have to do more calculations."

"Calculations?" Omni looked at her as if she were

crazy. "How's that gonna get us out of here?"

But Aja just began scribbling. As she furiously calculated, she realized her mistake. There were *two* sets of variables. The symbols and the *times* between reconfigurations. The time was anywhere between one and five minutes.

"Let's just *go!*" Omni grabbed her hand and started yanking. "How are we gonna get out if we don't explore?"

"Omni, please—"

"Let's *go*! I wanna *go*! I wanna go into another room. Why do we have to stop *here*?"

Her eyebrows went up. That was it! That was why Nak said he wasn't cheating. The times between the moves were a red herring! They were just random.

No, Lifelight reprogrammed the sequences depending on where you stopped. If you followed the symbols to the very end of the sequence, Lifelight would just start the next sequence. But if you didn't, if you stopped in a room that *wasn't* the final one in the sequence, then Lifelight would generate a new sequence—a sequence that was based on the symbol on the door of the room where you stopped. Which meant . . .

She began scribbling again.

"Let's go!" Omni pleaded.

"Wait!" she shouted. "Shut up!"

Omni fell on the floor and started to cry.

"Look, I'm sorry," she said. "I'm not trying to be mean. It's just that—"

She started running sequences as fast as she could. There had to be a way to get out. Nak said he wasn't a cheater. She had said that she was better in math. And he'd said, "Exactly!" Like that was somehow to his advantage. Like math wasn't the solution to the problem.

Surely it wasn't something stupid. Like she had to smash the wall down with a crowbar or something. No. Even if she had a crowbar, that wouldn't work. These walls were all too thick. It had to be something else. It had to be.

And then she knew what it was. Press had said that sometimes the solution was that there *wasn't* a solution. The solution wasn't math! Not exactly, anyway. It was . . . well . . . *anti*-math!

She smiled furtively. Then she started to scribble.

It took three more moves and a lot of calculation. But finally she did it. Once she found the sequence, she memorized it.

"Let's go, Omni," she said.

"Did you figure a way out?"

She shook her head. "Nope."

The boy looked at her hopelessly. "Then why go anywhere? My ankle hurts. I just wanna lie down."

"Can you trust me?" Aja's eyes bored into the boy's.

He nodded.

"All right then."

They began walking. They walked and walked and walked, following the sequence of symbols she'd memorized. Through reconfiguration after reconfiguration.

"When are we gonna get there?" Omni said after they'd gone through at least six or eight reconfigurations.

"We're almost there," Aja whispered.

The walls began grinding.

"This way," Aja said.

"But we've been in this same stupid room five times before. There's no way out from here."

"That's right," Aja said. "There's no way out from here."

They walked into the room. It was high ceilinged, with all kinds of scary carvings of the Beast chiseled into the walls.

"Now," Aja said. "Stop."

They stopped. For a moment, nothing happened.

And then, the carvings began to fracture, like reflections in a breaking mirror. A high-pitched whistle, like a terrible wind, filled Aja's head. The fractured images grew dim as the whistle grew louder.

And then—suddenly—there was nothing at all.

ELEVEN

Aja woke to find herself lying in the jump tube. Her head was aching. Her teeth were chattering. Her mind was a blur. What was happening?

She sat up slowly. All the lights were off and a strange low pulsing tone was echoing throughout the building. As she stumbled out into the hallway, she saw a red light on the wall flashing on and off.

Dazed-looking people were walking around in the hall.

"What happened?" a man said.

"I don't know," a young woman replied. "I was in the middle of a jump, and I heard this weird noise. . . ."

The lights blinked back on, the flashing red lights went off, and then a soothing voice broadcast: "Lifelight has experienced a brief break in service. All systems are now functioning properly again. However, all jumps will be temporarily suspended while diagnostic routines are implemented. Lifelight apologizes for the inconvenience."

She noticed Headmistress Nilssin standing near her booth, talking urgently on her communicator. She turned and looked curiously at Aja. "Something happened to Lifelight," she said.

And then it all came back to her.

"I just spoke to Dal from the core control room," Headmistress Nilssin said. "We had a stroke of amazing luck. There was a brief power failure and a total system shutdown. That's the first time it's happened in years. But when the system came back, the program was inactive. Dal's been able to quarantine it and erase it from the system."

"Good," Aja said.

Headmistress Nilssin looked at her closely. "Aja? Aja, are you okay?"

"Now that you mention it," Aja said, "I feel a little funny." Then her feet went out from under her and she slumped against the wall.

TWELVE

Aja Killian sat in Headmistress Nilssin's office. After her last jump she had spent three days in the hospital. But she was better. And now Headmistress Nilssin was welcoming her back to the academy.

"Did you find Omni?" Aja said.

The headmistress smiled. "Omni's fine. He was in a jump tube in a different level of the research wing." Her smile faded. "But we can't find Nak Adyms anywhere."

"I don't expect you will," Aja said. "Not anytime soon. With the skills he's got, he'll be able to disguise his identity anywhere he goes."

"I'm told that Nak hacked the origin code," the headmistress said. "If Lifelight hadn't had that temporary shutdown, you might well have died in his game. You're very lucky."

"No," Aja said. "Luck didn't have anything to do with it."

The headmistress frowned. "Meaning what?"

"The shutdown wasn't accidental."

The headmistress looked at her curiously.

"Say what you will about him, Nak didn't cheat. There was only one way out of the game. See, the maze was designed to reprogram itself based on where you went in it. But it followed a strict algorithm. The reprogramming of the maze was a solution to a mathematical sequence. Each time it reprogrammed, that would determine where you had to go if you wanted to get to the exit gate. The thing is, the exit gate was actually a tease, a diversion. It closed automatically before you could ever actually get out."

The headmistress cleared her throat. "I'm not sure I see what this has to do with—"

"Listen," Aja said. "Once I figured out that the route to the gate was a solution to a mathematical problem, and that the problem was based on which chambers you went into, I simply constructed a problem that the computer couldn't solve."

The headmistress's eyes widened. "Like a non-terminating, nonrepeating decimal!"

"Exactly. The same idea. It's possible to create a mathematical series that never ends. It just goes on and on and on forever. You see, in order to keep anybody from knowing what he was up to, Nak had to run his code in Lifelight's Alpha Core. His game had Priority One access to Lifelight's processing power, along with the ability to modify Lifelight's origin code. So once the program started trying to solve an unsolvable problem, Lifelight rechanneled one hundred percent of its processing power into solving the problem. Since the problem was unsolvable, it maxed out the system. Boom. Automatic shutdown."

Headmistress Nilssin looked at Aja for a long time. "Amazing."

"There *was* one strange thing though," Aja said. "Inside the game I ran into a man. A man named Press. He told me that he was tandeming into the game, but that Nak didn't know he was there."

"Press?" the headmistress said, eyes widening. "*Press* was inside the game?"

"You know him?"

Headmistress Nilssin smiled fondly. "Yes, I do."

"He told me all this weird stuff about how I was something called a 'Traveler.' It didn't seem like he was part of the game at all. He told me that he couldn't talk to me in person because there was some evil guy here. Some guy who was spying on me or something."

The headmistress's face went pale. "*What* evil guy?"

"Saint Something. Saint Pain, Saint Rain . . ."

"Saint *Dane*?"

Aja looked at her, puzzled. "Yeah. That's it. He said he was masquerading as that Lifelight director, Allik Worthintin."

The headmistress didn't say anything for a very long time. Then, finally, she reached into a desk drawer and pulled something out. "I've been holding something here that I probably should have talked to you about a long time ago," she said. "But . . . you push yourself so hard. I guess I just didn't want you to have *this* burden too. Not at such a young age."

"What burden?" Aja said. She had an odd feeling

rising inside her—the nervous, frightened feeling she got when things weren't working out the way she'd predicted.

Headmistress Nilssin leaned forward, rested one fingertip on the desk, and then pushed something across the wood toward Aja.

There, on the desk, lay a small silver ring with a stone in the center. Aja picked it up and examined it. Around its rim were strange little symbols.

"Unfortunately," the headmistress said, "it's not a game. Press is real. Everything he said to you in the game was true."

Aja swallowed.

"Before you take this ring," the headmistress said, "I have to ask you something. What have you learned from this experience?"

Aja squinted, thinking hard. "I've always thought that the solution to every problem could be found through logic. But I guess sometimes it can't. Sometimes you have to rely on other things. Feelings, emotions, whatever." She paused. "Remember when Allik Worthintin was trying to get me to go up to his office with him? There was a moment there where Dal Whitbred could have decided not to let me jump again. And yet ultimately he decided to trust me."

The headmistress nodded.

"I mean, honestly?" Aja said. "He didn't make the logical choice. Everything pointed to me being the person who was destroying the core. But I think he did it because he saw something in my eyes. Something he trusted. He made his choice based on a feeling."

Aja picked up the ring and studied the symbols. They were the same ones that had been carved into the rock inside the maze.

"I'm glad to hear you say that," the headmistress said. "The thing that has always worried me about you is that you put too much faith in logic. But now? Now I think you're ready."

"Ready for what?"

"There are a great many things I need to tell you, Aja." The headmistress put her hand on Aja's. "You see, I am the Traveler on Veelox. And you are my successor."

After her strange conversation with the headmistress, Aja walked out into the quad, her head in a whirl. So it was really true, the stuff that Press had said in the game? It just didn't seem to make sense. She felt like Lifelight must have felt, trying to process a problem that didn't have a logical solution. She wasn't used to feeling that way.

As she turned the corner, she bumped into a tall man.

"Sorry," she said.

The man stepped back. He had jet black hair and the palest blue eyes she'd ever seen. It was Allik Worthintin. A cold feeling ran down her spine. If everything Headmistress Nilssin had just said was true, then she was locked in a terrible struggle with this man.

You'd never have guessed it from the look on his face.

"No apology necessary, Aja," the man said pleasantly. Then he leaned toward her in a confidential manner.

"But in complete fairness, I should warn you. . . ." He spread his hands lightly.

"Warn me of what?" she said sharply.

Before turning and walking briskly away, the tall man smiled and gave her a broad wink. "The game," he said, "is only just beginning."

Elli Winter

ONE

"Run!"

Elli Winter was at the bottom of the six-foot-deep hole. Her shovel had just hit the box. She looked up to see what the commotion was about. Elli was a short woman, and the hole was so deep she couldn't really see anything. Just the blue, cloudless sky.

"Chopper!" somebody else shouted. "The dados are coming! Run!"

She could hear it then, the swoosh of the chopper blades over the horizon. She bent over and redoubled her efforts. Maybe she could get to the box before the security dados got there. She had a very strong feeling about this box. It was important. This was the last excav the team would ever do. She had to take a chance. She had to keep digging.

"Run!" Elli recognized the voice of the excav team leader, Olana Carlings. "Run for the trees!"

The hole was in the middle of a large meadow surrounded on both sides by small forested mountains.

She supposed Olana was right. If she ran now, there was a good chance of escaping into the wooded hills, where the dados would have trouble finding her.

Instead, though, she jammed the blade of the shovel into the soft earth, tipped it back. She could see the whole box move. It was a long thin box. Maybe. Just *maybe* she'd get to the contents in time.

Olana Carlings pulled out her binoculars as soon as she reached the tree line. Everyone in the team had made it to the tree line. Everyone, that is, except Elli.

Elli had just stayed there in the hole, digging away. Even now, from her high vantage point on the mountainside, Olana could see that Elli was ignoring the oncoming black chopper. Painted on its side was the unmistakable logo of Blok—the powerful corporation that controlled the entire territory of Quillan.

"What is she *doing*?" muttered Olana.

Another team member shook his head sadly as the chopper swooped down over the hole.

Olana squinted, trying to make out details in the wobbly viewfinder of the binoculars. Elli was calmly working at the clasp that held the box shut. "She's got the box. She's opening it."

As she spoke, four black ropes tumbled from the belly of the chopper above Elli Winter. Then four green-clad security dados appeared, grabbed the ropes, and began dropping from the sky.

"What a shame," the other team member said. "I guess that's the end of the road for the cleaning lady."

Two

Five Years Earlier

There is a road," a voice said.

"Huh?" Elli Winter said, looking up to see who was addressing her. The voice had broken her from the terrible thoughts that had been running around her brain.

A smiling man stood behind a counter at the back of the video arcade. "There is a road," the man said. "Even at the end of the road, a new road stretches out."

She cocked her head. "I'm sorry, are you talking to me?"

The man motioned to her with his finger. He was a tall, good-looking man, dressed in a strange bright costume. Most people on Quillan dressed in shades of gray, so it was a little shocking to see someone dressed in bright colors.

"You're in pain," the man said. "I can see that. You've suffered a terrible loss. A loved one perhaps?"

She stared blankly at the man. How could he know such a thing? She had just received the letter this morning. The final nail in the coffin that was her life. Her husband of twenty years, Marvek Winter, had died working in the tarz. Gentle husband, devoted father—the sweetest man she'd ever known. Now he was dead.

"My husband," she said simply.

"Yes." The man nodded and his smile saddened. "I know. You think you've come to the end of the road. You think that you can't take care of your daughter anymore. You think that you're of no use to anyone."

A part of Elli Winter's mind wondered how he knew this, how he knew it so exactly. A part of her was angry that he was invading her little bubble of pain. But Elli was a polite and mild woman. It was not in her nature to snap at people. So she simply said, "Yes. But . . . how did you know?"

The man pointed at the sign on his counter.

SD FORTUNES
SUPER-DUPER!!!!!!
LEARN YOUR FORTUNE—ONLY 6 CREDITS

"Oh," she said. "I'm sorry. I didn't know. I don't have any money. I can't pay you."

She turned and stumbled away.

"No problem!" The man's cheery voice pursued her as she hurried toward the door of the video arcade. "This one's free! On the house, compliments of SD Fortunes, a subsidiary of the Blok Corporation."

She pushed the lever opening the door and stumbled into the street.

She could still hear the man's cheery voice pursuing her as the door closed. "Even at the end of the road, there is a road!"

Elli Winter had never put into words the things that the man had said. But it was true. She had been like a sleepwalker for the past year, doing her best not to think about anything at all.

Until a year ago she had lived a perfect life. As perfect as anybody could have on Quillan, anyway. She had a good job working maintenance at the Blok building. Her husband too had a good job. Neither of them made much money. But they lived a stable, modest life. And they had Nevva, their beloved daughter. For the first ten years of their marriage, Elli had been told by the doctors that she would be unable to have children. Adopting children on Quillan was nearly impossible for people without lots of money. But then one day, a miracle had happened—a miracle that brought Nevva to them.

Nevva had been an extraordinary child from day one. And both she and Marvek had been devoted to the girl. When it had become clear that Nevva was unusually bright, Elli and Marvek had put every spare penny into sending her to the best schools. But schools on Quillan weren't free. And the better the school, the more it cost.

The school Nevva attended had just been too expensive for their small incomes.

So Marvek had started betting on the games. At

first he'd done well. But then, inevitably, his luck had changed. Finally, in desperation, Marvek had come to this very arcade. He'd placed the ultimate bet—betting his own life against the pile of debts he'd accumulated.

And he'd lost. Losing the ultimate bet meant being sent straight to the tarz, the power plants that supplied all of Quillan. They were poisonous places. To work there was a death sentence.

For the past year, since he'd lost the bet, Elli had gone on with her life. As long as Marvek was alive, she had held out a scrap of hope. Maybe things would get better. Maybe Blok would have mercy on him, let him come home.

It was a dream. But it was a dream that helped her get out of bed, comb Nevva's hair, make her lunch, send her off to school. But Elli knew that, like all dreams, it was empty. For a year she'd barely been able to look Nevva in the eye. She hadn't been able to love her the way a mother should love a child. Because every time she looked at Nevva, she thought; *If only you hadn't been here, Marvek would still be coming home from work every day, giving me a kiss, reading the paper, eating dinner, smiling, laughing. . . .* It wasn't Nevva's fault. But Elli couldn't help the thought coming into her mind.

What kind of mother would think a thing like that?

Well. The letter had come today.

The Blok Corporation Power Generation and Transmission Division regrets to inform you of the death of . . .

And that was the end. The end of all hope.

She had balled up the letter, thrown it in the trash, and then said to Nevva, "I have to take a walk, sweetheart. Keep working on your homework."

"Okay, Mom."

So trusting. Nevva trusted her mother completely. Elli didn't feel worthy of that trust.

And now she was here. Now Elli Winter was here, walking down the street. A cold wind was blowing. A loud clap of thunder split the air, and then a frigid, driving rain hit her.

The street was crowded with tense, tired-looking people in gray clothes. Elli forced her way through them. Around her the tall gray buildings pressed in.

Elli looked at her surroundings as though she had never seen this place before. Had it always been such a miserable, cheerless, gray, ugly place?

Suddenly she came to a halt. In front of her was a low pedestrian barrier. On the other side of that lay a huge pit. Just a few months ago there had been some buildings here. They must have blown them up. Now they were building a new structure.

A large sign read,

FUTURE HOME OF BLOK CORP FUN DIVISION THE FUN STARTS HERE!

The sign was cockeyed, one of the support posts hanging over the side, into the pit.

She stared in. From every direction huge streams of water flowed into the pit, turning it into a giant quagmire.

Several pieces of earthmoving equipment were digging in the center of the hole. Over on the far side, a swarm of grim-faced, exhausted men were clawing at the earth with shovels. But the deepening water had turned the dirt into mud. Every time they lifted out a shovelful of gray mud, more mud flowed back into its place.

Digging a hole that just filled itself back in. Her whole life seemed like this pit. A hopeless, pointless waste. If it weren't for Nevva . . .

Suddenly from the center of the pit came a scream. "Sinkhole! Sinkhole!"

A man, small as an ant, jumped from the seat of a giant earthmoving machine and started running. The mud came up to his thighs, so he seemed to be moving in slow motion.

"Run!" another man yelled. "Cave-in."

Then she heard it—a loud cracking noise. Something in the center of the pit had given way. A massive jagged hole opened up, like the snaggle-toothed mouth of some buried giant.

The men in the pit were abandoning their shovels, running panic stricken for the thin dirt path leading up to street level.

The mud and water began to flow toward the sinkhole. The pit became a huge vortex of water and mud circling down into the earth. Screams filled the air. The hole was widening. Earthmoving equipment toppled and sank into the hungry maw growing in the center of the pit.

Is this is it? Elli thought. *Is this is the end of the road?*

For reasons she couldn't quite express, she felt drawn toward the pit. She took a step forward. Then another.

Carefully she climbed the barrier. When she reached the edge, she stood as if hypnotized. Chunks of clay the size of cars began detaching from the side of the pit and falling in slow motion toward the bottom. Huge splashes of mud and water.

I should go back, she thought. *I really should.* But she didn't move.

Something gave way beneath her. And then Elli Winter was falling, the gray world pinwheeling around her.

THREE

Yellow sky. How strange.

The first thing Elli became conscious of was that the sky was yellow. She blinked.

"Look!" a voice said in a loud whisper. "She's conscious."

"Don't let her see your faces," another voice said. A man, harsh sounding.

Elli blinked. Not a sky after all. It was a ceiling. Who would paint a *ceiling* yellow? It was just the oddest thing.

She sat up, choked, coughed. Her mouth was full of dirt, and it felt as if there were water in her lungs.

It started coming back to her. She'd fallen into the pit. But after that? Nothing. Blackness. Blackness and the feeling of being carried along by water—spun, flipped, slammed into things.

"Where am I?" she said.

There were three of them. Two of them were covering parts of their faces with their shirts. The third, a very large man, wore a black mask. "Be quiet," the large man said harshly. "And don't move."

She frowned. Was this some kind of dream? She looked around. She seemed to be in some kind of warehouse. Long rows of shelves filled the immense space. One wall was splintered and twisted. A huge slick of mud had poured through it into the large room where she was lying.

"But . . . what happened?"

"One of the old subway tunnels under the city caved in. A bunch of water flowed through it and tore out the wall of our—"

"Quiet!" the large man shouted.

But it started coming back then. She remembered standing by the edge of the pit. Feeling it pulling her forward. Falling. Then blackness. Blackness and the feeling of being pulled down into the ground by the flowing mud.

The large man whispered to the others. "We can't let her . . ." He let his sentence die.

"Are you saying . . ." One of the others, a woman, spoke. She too couldn't seem to finish her sentence.

The third one, a smaller man, said, "What? You want to kill her? That what you're saying?"

The big man shrugged. "We have no choice. If we let her go, she'll talk to Blok's security people. There'll be dados blasting through the doors in an hour."

Silence.

"You know I'm right," the big man said.

It took Elli a minute to realize it: They were talking about her! And yet, somehow, she didn't really care. The end of the road. She'd come to the end of the road. Right?

The woman said, "Tylee will be here first thing in the morning. Let's let her decide."

"She can't go anywhere," the smaller man said. "Just leave her be. Tylee can decide."

"We have to evacuate now," the big man said. "If Blok's people come down that tunnel, they'll find us. We can't risk it."

"But we need to get this mess cleaned up!"

The man shook his head. "It won't do us any good to clean up a few boxes, and then lose half our people."

The two others nodded grudgingly.

The big man turned and looked at Elli. "This place is surrounded by guards. If you try to leave, they'll shoot you on sight. Clear?"

Elli nodded.

"Stay here. We'll be back in the morning."

The three turned and walked away. Their footsteps echoed hollowly and finally disappeared.

Elli stood up, looked fearfully around. There was still a disconcerting gurgle in her lungs that made her cough every few breaths. Her clothes were slick with mud. She shivered and wondered if there was someplace to clean up. She wandered around for a few minutes, looking at the warehouse. There were huge shelves running far off into the distance. Each shelf was lined with cheap cardboard boxes, some of which looked quite old.

Elli couldn't help wondering who these people were who had found her. They were obviously some kind of criminal organization.

But why would a criminal organization be guarding an underground building full of cheap boxes? She decided to take a peek into one of the boxes. Inside the box she found a stack of small paintings. Elli was no expert in art, but they appeared to be watercolors. She took one out and stared at it. She looked at the date in the bottom corner. It was over two hundred and fifty years old! But the colors were amazingly bright and vivid. It was a picture of a laughing girl in a bright-colored dress, playing in the middle of a field of flowers.

She had never seen anything like it. Something about it took her breath away. She looked at another box. More beautiful pictures. There was something about all of them—something so bright and colorful that they seemed almost to have come from another world. Another box. More beautiful pictures. Bright flowers in each one of them. Brilliant yellows, rich reds, deep blues and purples. A sense of peace and calm washed through her.

She looked around the area where the concrete wall had been ripped apart. Boxes were sprawled in heaps, covered in mud. With horror she realized that every single one of those boxes must have been full of the same kind of beauty she'd just seen. They would be ruined!

Elli crawled over the chunks of concrete and mud and started pulling boxes out of the mess. She had no awareness of time. She just felt impelled to save as much as she could.

Once she'd gotten the boxes out of the muck, she began opening them one by one. Sometimes the contents were completely ruined. After she'd carefully sorted through an entire box and found every single picture destroyed, she found herself bursting into tears.

What's gotten into me? she wondered.

Suddenly it struck her—she had no idea what time it was, how long she'd been working. Was it night or day? She had no clue.

The only thing she did know for certain was that her daughter, Nevva, was sitting at home wondering what had happened to her mother. The thought made her clench up inside. But Elli knew that even if she could have left this strange subterranean place, she couldn't have faced going home.

So she picked up another box and tried to put Nevva out of her mind.

With as much care as she could muster, she began cleaning the dirty pieces of paper. But she realized they needed to be dried. She wandered around the echoing building and found a room with some office supplies in it, including a roll of string.

She brought the string back, ran several strands from one shelf to another. If a painting was wet, she hung it to dry. Soon there were papers hanging everywhere overhead.

Elli worked and worked, cleaned and cleaned. The harder she worked, the more she cleaned, the better she felt. She felt as though she were cleaning her whole life away, leaving her old life behind.

Eventually her eyes grew gritty and her body became heavy with fatigue. But still she worked. If she slacked up for even a moment, so much of this beauty would be lost!

Finally, though, she couldn't put off the inevitable.

She sat down in a chair and slept. When she woke, her back and neck were stiff. She looked around. The mess was still considerable. It seemed as if she'd barely made a dent.

She began to work again. As she worked, she began to mutter little phrases to herself. Advertising jingles, silly little poems she'd read. All her life Elli had been able to memorize pretty much anything she read or heard, so her head was full of thousands of useless little words.

As she worked, she repeated them. Over and over and over.

"It's not just clean. It's Blok clean! It's not just clean. It's Blok clean!" That was an advertisement for a cleaning product she used at home. There were plenty of other phrases that stuck in her head. They kept her mind occupied, filled up, so that she could stop thinking about what a terrible mother she was, so she could stop wondering where Nevva was or how Nevva felt.

"It's not just clean. It's Blok clean! It's not just clean . . ."

And so it went for a long time. Elli Winter had no clear idea of how much time had passed. The big man in the mask had said that he and the others would return the next morning. But they didn't. And if there were guards anywhere, Elli never saw them.

No one came for a very long time. Maybe as much as a week. She had no clock, so she really couldn't know for sure.

And in all that time, she did nothing but work. She found some food in a refrigerator. So when she got hungry, she ate. Eventually she cleaned her clothes in the bathroom, washed the mud from her face, her hair, her fingernails. But otherwise, it was just work and sleep.

And then, suddenly, armed men were streaming through a door.

"Get down on the ground!" one of them screamed. "Down! Down! Down! Do it now!" So Elli lay down, splaying her arms across the cold concrete floor.

The end of the road. She'd put it off by a few days. But now it was finally here.

Well, she thought, *at least I saved some beautiful pictures.*

FOUR

Elli Winter lay staring across the floor as the masked men moved silently through the warehouse. She'd expected them to do something to her. But instead they more or less ignored her.

At first she had thought they were security dados. But they weren't. They were just normal people dressed in military-style clothes, black masks over their faces. They seemed to be searching for something.

Finally one of them spoke into a radio. "No sign of dados or bugs. Think it's safe for Tylee."

The masked men stood around silently for a while. Elli lay motionless. Words and phrases ran through her head. *It's not just clean. It's Blok clean! It's not just clean. It's—*

Then, finally, a thin woman appeared in the nearest doorway and walked toward Elli. She was the first unmasked person Elli had seen in the warehouse. There was something special about the woman. It was unmistakable. She had an aura of authority, of command. Everyone seemed to straighten up as soon as they saw her.

The woman paused, studied the entire area carefully.

"Who did this?" she demanded finally, waving her hand around her. Elli took it all in for the first time. The floor was spotless. The concrete chunks had been hauled away. The mud was gone. And every single picture that had been salvageable was now hanging in one of the hundreds of lines crisscrossing the air above her head. Remembering the incredible mess that had been here before, Elli was almost amazed at what she'd accomplished.

"I did," she said softly.

Tylee frowned. "I was told this place was completely wrecked," she said to one of the masked men.

"It was," the man said, sounding a little puzzled. Elli recognized him as the big man who'd left her here before.

"Get up," the woman said.

Elli sat up. She felt woozy and unstable, as if she were coming out of a dream. A forest of color hung above them.

"You did *all* of this?" the woman said.

Elli nodded. "I'm sorry," she said.

"Sorry?" The woman cocked her head, curious.

"I shouldn't have touched anything," Elli said.

"Why? Why did you do all this?"

Elli frowned. She wasn't sure. She hadn't thought it through, really. She'd just *done* it. She looked up at all the bright-colored pictures above her. Her voice finally came out, haltingly. "It's just—they were so beautiful. I didn't want—I didn't want the world to lose all that beauty."

The woman had deep brown eyes. Suddenly they seemed very warm. She nodded and smiled sadly. "Yes. That's exactly it, isn't it?"

Elli sat on the floor and looked up at the forest of brightly colored paper above her head. She felt a warm sensation of satisfaction filling her chest. Other than taking care of Nevva, this was really the first thing she'd done in her life that seemed to have any meaning.

"My name is Tylee," the woman said to Elli.

"Do you mind my asking what this place is?" Elli said.

"It's a storehouse," Tylee said. "All the things that have happened on Quillan, all the writings of the ancients, all our history, all our music and art and science and inventions—everything that we Quillans were before Blok—it's all stored here."

Elli felt puzzled. "For what?"

"We are revivers," Tylee said. "Someday we will rise up out of this place and destroy Blok. We're keeping it all for the time that comes after. For the revival."

"Oh," Elli said.

Revivers! She had heard of them before. Only in whispers, though. A strange group that sought to destroy the established order and bring chaos to the world. That's what people said, anyway. Mad bombers, crazed lunatics, criminals, bandits, killers!

Except . . . these people didn't seem that way. If they were trying to save all this beauty, Elli reflected, then how bad could they be?

"I can't let you leave here," Tylee said. "You understand that, don't you?"

Elli shrugged. "I don't want to leave," she said softly.

"You *what*?" the big man in the mask said.

Elli shook her head. "I have nothing. My life out

there . . ." She pointed at the great gash in the concrete wall. "My life out there is over. I'm at the end of the road."

"You can't just *stay* here!" the big man growled.

"I like to clean," Elli said. "I could clean."

The big man looked at Tylee. "Come on, Tylee! I'm sure she's a nice lady and everything. But someday she'll destroy this place. We don't even know her name."

"Maybe we don't need to," Tylee said.

"I like to clean," Elli said again.

"We have guards. We have archivists. We have a lot of people here. We'll keep an eye on her."

"Tylee—"

"I've made my decision, Bart!" Tylee snapped. "If we kill her, we're no different from Blok. She stays. That's final."

The big man shook his head in disgust.

"We needed a cleaning lady down here anyway," Tylee said. She surveyed the damaged wall. "Now let's get people in here and fix that wall."

"Yes, ma'am," the big man said.

Tylee clapped her hands. "Now, people! Do it now!"

The people in the room began stripping off their masks. Soon everyone was hustling and bustling around.

Elli stood watching them.

I guess I should do something, she thought. She walked around until she found a janitor's closet. There was a broom leaning against a shelf full of cleaning products that looked as if they hadn't been touched in decades.

She picked up the broom and began to sweep.

FIVE

Elli Winter's life quickly fell into a routine. Each morning she got up and showered. For the rest of the day, she cleaned. After she ate supper, she found a book to read. One section of the warehouse was basically a library, with thousands—maybe even millions!—of old books.

The revivers called the warehouse "Mr. Pop." Which seemed like an odd name. But Elli Winter was not the kind of person to question other people's judgment.

The books Elli read told about a world that was very different from the one in which she lived. It was hard to put into words . . . but the people in the books seemed to live lives of greater intensity.

Then, after she got tired, she went into the broom closet to sleep. She had a small cot, her head next to the rack of cleaning products. Other than her clothes, she only had one personal possession. She had a worn picture of Nevva that had been in her pocket when she was swept through the collapsed tunnel. She had leaned Nevva's picture against a bottle of Blok Super-Duper Floor Cleaner.

Each night before turning off the light, she kissed the tattered photo. And then she slept.

Elli didn't talk much. There were actually a lot of people who worked in the warehouse. They all wore green aprons and took care of the things that were stored there. The green-aproned caretakers spoke in hushed voices. None of them were unfriendly to her. But they were all slightly distant. She was different from them. She knew it and they knew it. They had all chosen to come here. Their very presence was a testimony to their courage, their belief, their strength. She, on the other hand, was here because she was weak and cowardly, because she couldn't face the world.

So she didn't mind that no one really spoke to her. "I'll just sweep over there, if that's all right, dear," she'd say. Or, "If you don't mind, I'll just sneak in here and get your trash."

After a while she heard them referring to her as "the cleaning lady." It pleased her somehow to have no name, to pass almost invisibly, like a ghost, among them.

One day—not terribly long into her life in the warehouse, though time was difficult to measure there—a group of men and women was milling around near the main exit to the building. It was nighttime and the warehouse was empty. Most of the caretakers only came in during the day.

"Where's Gaff?" an athletic-looking woman said.

"He should have been here by now," a tall man with red hair replied.

"We can't wait any longer," the athletic-looking woman added.

"But if we're short a team member—," the tall man said.

"This excav is important," the athletic woman said. She seemed to be the leader of the group. "We've got to do it."

Elli had heard people talking about excavs. But she had no idea what they were. And she didn't ask. It wasn't her place. Besides, secrecy was important here. Nobody used their real name. That way if the dados showed up someday, you couldn't give up the names of any of your fellow revivers.

"We can't do it if we're short a team member," a dark-haired man said. Elli recognized him as Bart, the large man who'd discovered her when she first washed into Mr. Pop.

"So call off the excav," another man said.

"No way," the athletic woman said. "Find a way, Bart."

"Look, I'm responsible for the digging, Olana," the dark-haired man said. "And I'm telling you, we can't do it. Not with the time limits we're dealing with now. I need four people on shovel duty, or I'm not going. That's final."

Bart and Olana. Elli had heard the names before in connection with the excavs. But this was the first time she had seen Olana.

"What about her?" the red-headed man said, pointing at Elli.

Elli blinked. The people standing by the door all turned and looked at her.

"Who . . . the *cleaning lady*?" Olana said skeptically.

"Why not?" Bart said. "I hear she works hard."

"Somebody told me she's not allowed to leave here," the fourth person said.

"That was a long time ago," Bart said. "We need a digger."

Olana shrugged. "You're okay with it, I'm okay with it." She snapped her fingers at Elli. "Hey! Cleaning lady. Wanna go on an excav?"

Elli walked tentatively toward the group. "Um . . . probably it would be best if—"

"Can you use a shovel?" Bart said. "Can you dig?"

"Well—sure, I guess, but—"

"That's all we need to know," Olana said. "Blindfolds on. Let's go!"

The next thing she knew, one of the team members had slapped a black hood over her head. Now someone was leading her out the door.

Wait! Elli wanted to scream. *I'm not supposed to do this! I'm not approved to leave the warehouse.*

But it was too late. She was in some sort of vehicle, tearing along at top speed. "Stay low," a voice said. "Stay low and don't talk."

Elli hunched down in her seat.

They drove silently for a long time. Suddenly the vehicle stopped.

"Hoods off!" a female voice called.

Elli pulled off the itchy black hood. She was in the back of a truck. Everyone was jumping off onto the ground. She followed.

They were obviously not in the city anymore. They

were *way* into the country now. A huge old house—a castle almost—stood to their left. Its roof had collapsed, but the stone walls still stood. There was a full moon overhead and very few clouds. It was bright enough to see clearly. Elli had not been to the country since she was a little girl. Most people on Quillan lived in the cities and didn't venture into the country very often. She found it quite frightening.

"Let's go, guys!" the team leader, Olana, called. "Hustle, hustle."

They walked single file toward the spooky-looking old building. "So, um, what exactly are we doing?" Elli said.

Bart explained. "We've been assembling historical and cultural artifacts at Mr. Pop for many years now. When Blok first started taking over Quillan, they began to suppress anything that conflicted with Blok. At first they only suppressed political writing that attacked Blok. Then they suppressed weapons. But soon they began to grow afraid of anything they couldn't control. Art, music, poetry, advertisements—you name it. They started suppressing everything. So people began burying books, paintings, sculptures, recordings. The earliest revivers were part of this movement to preserve our culture. Once Mr. Pop was established, we began going back and digging up our treasures."

Elli started to get it now. "Excavations," she said.

"Right. Now we just call them 'excavs.'"

As they walked into the old building, Elli smiled. "So we're here to dig up buried treasure?" she said.

"Kind of like that, yeah," Bart said.

"So how do we know where to find the stuff?" She looked around the inside of the old mansion or castle or whatever it was. The roof had collapsed. There was old furniture here and there, rotted out, covered with vines. A small tree grew in the middle of the building.

"We have maps," Olana chimed in. "Sometimes they're good. And sometimes—"

Bart held up an ancient, yellowed piece of paper. "And sometimes they're like *this*."

Olana clicked on a flashlight, directed it at the paper. It was a crudely drawn map of the building with a red "X" drawn in one corner.

"There are the stairs down," Bart said, pointing. In the far wall was a small stone doorway. The group walked to it and began to descend a spiral stair leading down. Elli could feel her heart thumping. She had never been anyplace like this before. It was very dark and chilly. Spider webs hung from the low stone ceiling.

A few moments later the stair came out into a large cryptlike space with a dirt floor and arched stone roof.

Olana scratched her head and looked at the map. "Oh, man," she said. "This place is bigger than I thought."

Elli could feel an odd tingling in her limbs. She was frightened by the strange place. But there was something . . . For a moment she couldn't put her finger on it. Then she realized. She was *excited*! That's what it was. She hadn't felt this way for . . . well, she couldn't really remember. It had been years and years and years. It was the feeling of doing something wrong, something forbidden.

She remembered once in her youth sneaking off to

a park with a boy. They'd taken off their shoes and played in a creek. They'd been caught and punished severely. But she could still remember the feel of the water running across her feet. The feeling of freedom. The feeling of—

"We'll start digging over there," Bart said.

"No," Olana said. "It says to dig right here." She pointed to another location.

"You've got the map backward," Bart said.

"No, *you* do!"

It was obvious to Elli by now that Bart and Olana didn't get along all that well. Elli looked around the room, thinking about where she would have buried something here if it had been her most valuable possession.

Not in either of the places that Bart and Olana were suggesting that they dig.

"May I?" she said, holding out her hand for the map.

Bart and Olana looked at her irritably. "You're here to dig, okay?" Bart said. "No offense, but we're the experts."

"Okay," Elli said mildly. But in the back of her mind, she knew that she knew something. She wasn't sure what it was. But she knew where to dig.

There were four diggers—Elli, Bart, and the two other strong-looking men.

Bart walked over to one corner of the crypt or basement or whatever it was and drew a square on the ground with his toe.

"I'm not sure—," Elli said.

"Look, it's Olana's job to get us here and back. It's my

job to figure out where to dig. It's your job to dig where I tell you. Clear?"

Elli smiled and nodded. But she felt quite sure they were digging in the wrong place.

They started working. While they dug, Olana paced around nervously, looking at her watch. Every now and then Bart would say, "Faster. Dig faster."

"I'm not trying to be difficult, but what's the rush?" Elli said.

"We used to be able to take our time," Olana said. "But Blok security is on to us now. We don't know how. Tracking devices, spies—we're just not sure. But somehow they've managed to close in on us. And they get closer all the time."

Bart paused in his digging and wiped his brow. "Right now we seem to have about a five-hour window before the security dados show up. Just in case they get here quicker, though, we've got lookout teams around us. If they spot trouble, we run."

Olana nodded. "Which reminds me," she said. "If the dados come, we don't wait. We drop everything and we go. We have ten seconds to get in the truck and go. Understood?"

Elli nodded.

"Ten seconds. Not eleven. We're in that truck and we're gone. We don't wait. If you hang around, you're left behind. Period. Understood?"

Elli nodded.

Olana stared down into the hole they'd been digging. It was all the way up to Elli's waist now. Her arms were exhausted from the digging.

"We're digging in the wrong place," Olana said, shaking her head skeptically. "They never bury anything this deep."

"That's not true," Bart said. "Once we found—"

"Okay, so *once* we had to dig five feet down. I'm telling you, Bart, this is the wrong—"

Bart sighed loudly. "If you're such a genius, where *should* we dig?"

"Over . . . uh . . . over there," Olana said, not sounding very certain.

"Exactly *where* over there?"

"Well, you know, the 'X' on the map is uh, generally, uh—"

"We could be a foot off," Bart said. "It could be right here." He kicked the dirt by his foot.

The other diggers began muttering irritably. It was obvious everyone was growing impatient and nervous.

"We've got three hours," Olana said. "That gives us time for one more hole. Where's it gonna be?"

"We'll just expand this one," Bart said.

"I think we should—"

"No!" Elli was startled to hear her own voice coming out loudly and confidently.

Everyone turned and looked at her.

"Excuse me?" Olana said.

"Let me see the map," Elli said.

Olana frowned, but handed it to her. The map only confirmed what Elli had been thinking since she walked down into this basement. She climbed out of the hole and began walking slowly to the opposite wall, scanning the ground with her flashlight.

Finally she stopped. She really wasn't sure why she knew. But she knew. This was the place.

"Here," she said.

Bart snorted. "Oh great! So after a couple hours of digging, the cleaning lady has become an expert excavator."

The man's sarcasm didn't bother her. "See?" she said, pointing at the moldy dirt below them. "There's a depression here. Somebody dug it out, then refilled it."

"This was buried over a hundred and fifty years ago," Olana said. "I don't think some little depression in the dirt would last a hundred and fifty years."

"The map very clearly shows this isn't the right place," Bart said. "See how—"

Suddenly Olana's radio squawked.

"We've got visitors!" Olana shouted.

"Back to the truck!" Bart shouted. "Go, go, go!"

The other excav team members went storming up the stairs. But for some reason, Elli couldn't move. She felt rooted to the spot. She knew that they had said she only had ten seconds to get to the truck. But . . .

Dig! she thought. *I have to dig!*

It was here. Right here. She was sure of it.

Finally, though, she ran up the stairs. By the time she made it to the top, she could hear the truck engine starting. As she ran out the front door of the ruined building, she saw the truck tearing off into the distance, disappearing into the woods.

She'd waited too long. The ten seconds were up. They'd left her.

"Oh, dear," she said mildly. What was she going to do?

She stood for a moment in the silence. The moon was

tangled up in the limbs of the trees now, and long black shadows crisscrossed the ground.

For the second time this night, she felt afraid. Alone and afraid. She was shivering, and her heart banged in her chest.

Suddenly a shadow separated itself from the other shadows. The shadow became a man, his face hidden in blackness. He had something in his hand, a long sticklike thing. It looked like a weapon of some sort.

"Your shovel," the man said, holding out the weapon. "You dropped your shovel, Elli."

Six

Elli peered at the man. He came closer, and his face became visible for the first time, lit now by the moon. He was smiling at her as if he were sharing some kind of joke with her. There was something familiar about him.

"Even at the end of the road, Elli," he said, "there is a road."

It came back to her then. The fortune-teller! He was the man in the fortune-telling booth!

"How do you know my name?" she whispered. Her heart was fluttering wildly.

"I know a lot about you," he said. "I even know some things about you that you don't know about yourself."

She frowned. "Who are you?"

"My name is Press," he said. "I've been trying to find you for quite a while. It never occurred to me that you were down there in Mr. Pop."

Mr. Pop! He even knew about Mr. Pop! Her head whirled with confusion.

"Are you with Blok security?" she said.

The man named Press laughed loudly. "Not even hardly."

"Then who are you?"

"That's a long story," he said. "The more important question is, *Who are you?*"

"I'm afraid I don't understand."

"Elli," he said, "your friends will be back in an hour or so. We don't have much time. So listen carefully. You are not who you think you are. You are a Traveler. . . ."

The man named Press talked to Elli for a long time, telling her all kinds of things that seemed completely far fetched and unbelievable. People who could travel through time and space. Civilizations on other territories. An epic battle of good and evil. A demon named Saint Dane. Quigs. Flumes.

It all sounded . . . well . . . insane, actually.

And when he explained to Elli that she was one of these special people who was destined to do all these big things as part of some giant universal conflict? Well . . . come *on*.

Finally Elli burst out laughing.

"Okay, okay, okay, stop," she said finally. "This is some kind of practical joke, isn't it? Do you guys do this to everybody on their first excav mission?"

Press shook his head, then reached into his pocket and pulled out a small silver ring. He held it out in his palm. Around the rim of the ring were tiny letters written in some kind of script that Elli had never seen before. They should have been invisible in the dark. But they weren't. They glowed slightly.

"Normally each Traveler is trained and given this ring by his or her predecessor," Press said. "But on Quillan things have worked out a little differently."

Elli looked closely at the ring. She had never seen anything that glowed like that. Certainly not a piece of metal. If this was all a joke, somebody had sure gone to a lot of trouble.

"Take it," Press said.

Elli kept looking at the glowing ring.

He was really serious, she realized finally. This wasn't a joke.

"Take it, Elli," Press repeated. "It's yours."

Finally Elli shook her head. "No," she said. "It's not for me. I'm not a courageous person. I'm a cleaning lady."

"I know what you've gone through," Press said. "I know that you feel like you've done a terrible thing by leaving your daughter without—"

Elli felt a flash of anger. "No, you don't!" she said. "You have no idea what it's like!"

Press was still holding out the ring. "Okay. Fair enough. But being a Traveler doesn't mean you're a super-hero. It doesn't mean you're flawless. It just means—"

Elli Winter stood and shook her head. "I'm sorry. I'm just not the kind of person you think I am. You say that each Traveler has a successor, right?"

Press nodded.

"Then let it be Nevva. She's stronger and smarter and more courageous than I could ever be."

Press's fingers closed slowly around the ring. He looked thoughtful. "Quillan *is* a special case," he said, almost to himself. "Perhaps . . ." He frowned.

"I'm sorry," she said. "I have work to do." She turned to go back down into the crypt.

"Wait."

She stopped and looked back at the man, his face half concealed in shadow.

"Here," he said. "Why don't you hold on to this, just in case." He handed her the ring. "No promises, just take the ring, keep it safe. And also, let me give you this." He reached into his pocket, stepped forward, and put something around her neck. She looked down. It was a necklace made of odd little beads. In the center was a slightly larger bead made from a gold-colored metal.

"Don't tell Nevva I'm alive," she said, fingering the strange necklace. "Let her think that I'm dead. Let her think that I'm a hero. Sometimes a lie is better than the truth."

"And sometimes a lie is not a lie," Press said.

Elli felt weary. She supposed that he was a good man, well intentioned. But the world seemed too complex when he was talking. Things were easier when you were cleaning.

Or digging.

"Good-bye, Elli," Press said. Then the strange man turned and melted away into the darkness.

An hour later she heard noises above her—rapid, determined footsteps. Dados? She wasn't sure. As long as she'd been digging, she felt okay. As soon as she'd stopped, though, she felt afraid. So she ignored the footsteps and kept digging.

Moments later the excav team bustled into the crypt

from the spiral staircase. Their flashlights probed the darkness.

"She's still here," Bart said, his beam coming to rest on Elli as she leaned deep into the hole.

"False alarm, Elli," one of the diggers said. "Turned out the watchers had spotted a herd of farm animals."

"I know you're probably upset that we left you," Olana said, "but we told you very clearly that we couldn't—"

She broke off. Elli looked up from the hole. The excav team stared as she lifted a small metal box free from the dirt and set it down gently on the ground.

"Oh my gosh," Olana said. "She found it."

"It was right where she said it would be," one of the other diggers added wonderingly.

There was a moment of stunned silence.

Elli climbed out of the hole and dusted off the dirty knees of her pants. She was not a pushy person. But sometimes she just knew something.

"I think it would be best if you brought me on the next excav," she said.

SEVEN

When the excav team got back to Mr. Pop, a team of green-smocked caretakers took the dirt-smeared old box.

"Could I . . ." Elli hesitated. "Could I see what we found?"

The senior caretaker looked at her curiously, then laughed. "Of course. Follow us."

They took the box to a room far in the back of the warehouse and carefully opened it. The box was made of some kind of silvery metal. On the inside it was perfectly clean. In fact, it looked as though it might have been packed that morning. Inside was a book.

There was an intake of breath by all the caretakers surrounding the box.

"What?" Elli said.

The senior caretaker reached in with white-gloved hands and gently removed the book from the box. "It's *The Book of Five Runes*," the senior caretaker said. He stared at it. "Oh, my!" he said. And then he kept saying it. "Oh, my! Oh, my! Oh, my goodness! Oh, my!"

Elli looked from face to face to face. "What's so special about this book?" she said.

The senior caretaker smiled and wiped his face. "We thought this one was gone forever. It's a very important book."

"What's it about?" Elli said.

The caretaker raised one eyebrow. "Well, actually, we're not sure. But many of the ancient writers refer to it." He held it out to her. "You found it. You could be the first to read it, if you'd like."

Elli felt uncomfortable with all the people looking at her. "Oh, no, I couldn't. I'm just the cleaning lady. I wouldn't even know what I was reading."

The caretaker shrugged, then handed the book to the head librarian. "Dr. Pender, I'll leave it in your care then."

Elli walked away from the group and began sweeping the floor. When she looked up again, no one was looking at her. They seemed to have forgotten she even existed.

At the end of the day, Elli realized that she had made a mistake. She had found the book, hadn't she? She should have at least looked at it. Not that she was worthy to actually *read* it. But maybe it would be okay to touch it. Maybe something about the extraordinary book would rub off on her.

Hesitantly she approached the head librarian, Dr. Pender, who was cleaning up his desk, as he was about to leave for the day.

"Excuse me," she said. "May I talk to you?"

Dr. Pender was a young man, already balding, with

only a fringe of blond hair around his head. He had always been pleasant to her. Like her, he was a shy man, and even though they had both been working at Mr. Pop together for several years, she had never really had a conversation with him. Dr. Pender looked up and smiled. "Of course, of course," he said, gesturing to a battered chair next to his desk. "Please, sit."

"Oh, no, that's all right."

"You're, uh . . . forgive me, I don't know your name. You're the cleaning person, right?"

Elli nodded. She felt tongue-tied now that she was with him.

"What is it?" he said.

"How do we know which books are important?" she said.

"Well . . ." He rubbed his face, then grinned. "That's a really good question! I guess there arc some books that affect lots of people. They affect how we think, what we believe, what we know. Other writers and thinkers refer to them. The great books, in a way, are what built Quillan."

"Oh," she said.

Dr. Pender cocked his head. "Was there something else?"

"Where are they?"

"You mean, where in the warehouse?"

She nodded.

"Follow me," he said. He walked out of his office and down the hallway to a small room that was separate from the main warehouse. He opened the door and pointed inside. She poked her head tentatively into the room.

The walls were lined with cheap shelves, sagging

under the weight of the books they contained. The volumes were mostly very old, some of them water damaged or moldy, some of them full of worm holes, some missing their covers. They didn't look important at all.

"Huh," Elli said.

"They don't look like much, do they?" the man said. "But they're very powerful. That's why Blok banned them all."

Elli stared at them. She felt intensely curious now. Before she came to Mr. Pop, she had never known anyone who was interested in books. No one ever talked about books on the popular video shows. The only books she had read as a child were the ones officially sanctioned— *The Happy Children*, *Garden of Fun*, *Champion Fighter*, *Best of the Best*, things like that. She could still remember all of them, could recite whole passages from them. But they hadn't seemed interesting to her. She could hardly muster any enthusiasm for them.

"Would it be possible . . ." She couldn't quite bring herself to finish the question.

"Would you like to read some of them?"

She nodded. "I mean—if it's not a problem."

Dr. Pender smiled. "That's what they're for, after all. To be read."

That night Elli went into the room where the special books were kept. She walked around for a long time, afraid to touch them, looking at the titles. Many of them were written in languages that she didn't understand. Finally she let her finger graze the spine of one of them. It was as though something electric had run up her arm.

Finally, after a long time, she selected one. It was a small book with a simple title. *The Underground Spring.*

She took it back to her room and began reading.

It was totally different from anything she'd read before. Most of the books she read were simple stories about women who fell in love or people who solved crimes or fought bad guys. But this book wasn't like that. It was about a man who went down into a cave and encountered a race of creatures who mined for jewels deep under the ground. After a while the man lost the ability to speak. Finally, after a very long time, he came back up out of the ground and found that everything he had known about—all the people, all the cities, all the buildings—was gone.

It didn't really make sense to her.

But she knew there was something going on under the surface of the story. Like a puzzle. If only she could figure it out.

Suddenly she realized that it was morning. She'd been reading all night. Hadn't slept for even a single second.

She fixed her breakfast, stumbled bleary eyed to the pushcart where she kept her mops and brooms, and began cleaning.

As she worked, she found herself reciting the entire book from memory. It was something she had always been able to do—a completely useless skill. But now, it seemed comforting to her. If she kept reciting the words, she thought, she might discover their meaning.

That night she fell asleep reading another strange book that didn't seem to make much sense. But the next day when she started working, she found herself repeating the whole book as she cleaned. The words that had seemed so puzzling the night before—well, they weren't *completely* clear yet. But they seemed a little easier to understand as they rolled off her tongue.

Sometimes as she mumbled the words to herself, a picture of her daughter, Nevva, would appear in her mind. In the past this had only made her feel sad. But now, as she repeated the ancient words, she felt better. It was as though the words somehow connected her to her daughter.

She realized that something had changed. Something inside her. But what it was, she wasn't really sure.

A week later one of the diggers from the excav team broke his leg. Olana and Bart had to make a special request to Tylee to add Elli temporarily to the team. But they got approval.

Next thing she knew, Elli was in the back of a van, hood over her head, riding along a rutted road. As they drew closer to the excav site, she felt a strange sense of peace inside.

The excav was done in daylight, in the middle of a huge field of grain. Robotic harvesters were moving through the fields, slowly cutting down the grain. As far as the eye could see, there was nothing but the tall stalks of grass on which the grain grew.

There were no trees, no buildings, no landmarks at all.

Bart and Olana were scratching their heads as they looked at the old map.

"There's supposed to be a tree here," Bart said. "The map shows a tree."

"The map's a hundred years old, Bart," Olana said. "They probably cut down the tree years ago."

Bart shook his head, looking disgusted. "This is a waste of time," he said.

The other diggers were scanning the horizon nervously. "I don't like this place," one of them said. "If the dados come, we've got nowhere to go."

A robotic harvester was lumbering slowly toward them. "I don't like that thing," the other digger said.

"May I see the map?" Elli said.

"Please do," Bart said, handing her the map.

She stared at it for a moment. It showed three hills, a tree, and a dirt road. She scanned the area. The hills and the dirt road were still there. She started walking toward the point where it seemed like the tree ought to be. But as she walked, she got the strongest feeling she was going the wrong way.

So she turned and walked in another direction. The long stalks of grain brushed against her legs. The sun was warm on her face. As she walked, she felt something on her neck. It seemed like the necklace that Press had given her was growing warmer. But maybe it was the sun. It was hard to tell.

She stumbled. There was something there! A little lump in the ground. She kicked the ground with her foot. And then smiled. It was the rotted stump of a tree, invisible unless you were standing right on top of it.

"Here," she said. "The cleaning lady says we dig here."

Bart and Olana looked at each other. Bart shrugged.

"Okay," Olana said. "We dig here."

Two hours later they were loading a dirty metal box into the van.

"So," Bart said as they settled down onto the van. "How'd you do it?"

"I just looked at the map, dear," Elli said with a shy smile.

Bart shared a glance with Olana. Then he turned back to Elli. "I think you should be a permanent member of the team. You okay with that?"

Elli hesitated. She could feel something lift and soar inside her chest. "Yes," she said finally. "I am."

EiGH+

Over time Elli read more and more of the books in the library. As she absorbed them into her brain, she found that they started to make a little more sense. She found writers who referred to other writers and other schools of thought. Things started adding up, making sense. But there was one thing that continued to puzzle her.

Finally she approached Dr. Pender and said, "I keep finding references to this book called '*The Analects of Kelln.*' Where is it stored? I can't seem to find it."

Dr. Pender shook his head sadly. "As far as we know, the last copy of the *Analects* was seized and burned over a hundred years ago."

"But it seems like it influenced—"

"You're exactly right." Dr. Pender finished her thought. "It's the central book in all ancient thought. The keystone, you might say. It influenced everything."

"And we've never found it?"

"We keep hoping that one of the excavs will locate it. But so far, we've been unlucky."

"What's it about?"

"*The Analects of Kelln*—so far as we can know—was a book of great hope. It was a book about change. You see, hope is based on the idea that the world changes, that things can get better. Blok hates change. Blok wants you to think that things are as good as they can possibly get. If people can change, if the world can change—well, then maybe we wouldn't need Blok anymore."

"I see," Elli said.

And from that moment she knew that, more than anything, she wanted to read that book.

As Elli worked that day, she thought about what Dr. Pender had said. Hope. She had put the whole idea of hope out of her head for a long time. Sometimes she found articles in the newspapers about her daughter. LOCAL GIRL NAMED BLOK STUDENT OF THE YEAR. TEENAGER WINS SCHOLARSHIP. WINTER ACCEPTS PRESTIGIOUS AWARD FOR SECOND YEAR RUNNING. That sort of thing. She would cut them out and paste them on the wall of the broom closet where she slept.

She felt hope for her daughter. Things might turn out well for Nevva. But for herself? Well . . . hard to say. Elli had to admit, she had begun to look forward to things. She looked forward to going on excavs. Getting out of the dull, windowless atmosphere of the warehouse was always a treat. She looked forward to reading every night. She looked forward to her occasional conversations with Dr. Pender.

But beyond that? Well, beyond that, it was hard

to see much further. She still couldn't imagine a life beyond this—living underground, cleaning, reading, eating, sleeping.

Over time she began to perceive a change in the mood of the people at Mr. Pop. They were more worried about the dados. More worried that Blok's security division was getting closer to finding them.

And the excavs were getting harder and harder to pull off. The security dados were arriving after only a couple of hours now.

In fact, there were rumors that Tylee was going to shut down the excav operations completely.

Then one day it happened. As she and the other excav team members arrived triumphantly at Mr. Pop with their latest discovery, they found Tylee standing at the entrance waiting for them, arms crossed.

"What is it?" Olana said.

Tylee's angular face showed no emotion. "You have all done fine work," she said. "Every reviver appreciates your service. But the time has come."

"Wait a minute!" Bart said.

"I'm sorry," Tylee said. "It's just too dangerous."

"It's just a matter of adjusting our tactics!" Olana added. "We just have to—"

Tylee held up her hand, cutting them off. "The decision has been made. We've worked too hard to accumulate all of this." She made a sweeping motion with her hand. "We can't jeopardize it just to add a few last trivial items."

"Trivial seems like the wrong word," Bart said combatively.

"In fact, Tylee, I hadn't had a chance to mention it," Olana added, "but in our last find, there was another map. It refers to several 'important items.'"

"What items?"

"It doesn't say, but—"

"Then it could be anything, couldn't it? Things that seemed important a hundred years ago sometimes don't seem so important today," Tylee said.

Elli spoke for the first time. "But sometimes they do."

Everyone turned and looked at her. They weren't used to hearing her speak. "Pardon me?" Tylee said. "You have something to add?"

Elli wasn't sure quite why she'd spoken. The necklace that Press had given her felt uncharacteristically hot against her skin. "I don't know exactly," she said timidly. "It's just—I feel as though this one's important."

"You *feel*?" Tylee said sharply.

Elli flushed. She really had no logical explanation. "I don't—I just feel like we should really find out what's there."

"You keep saying that you *feel*. Do you have any evidence? Do you have any information?"

Elli said nothing.

"All right then," Tylee said. "It's settled. I'm sorry. You have all done magnificent work. But now our movement must pass into a different phase."

Tylee turned briskly and walked away, her heels clicking sharply on the concrete.

The team members stared glumly after her.

"It's not right," one of the diggers said after Tylee had disappeared.

"I knew it was coming," Olana said. "But you always think there will be one more, you know?"

Heads nodded.

"There will be," Elli said softly.

Nine

It took Elli several weeks to work up the courage. Several weeks and a certain amount of planning. Among the many documents held in the warehouse were old maps of the city. She had to study them for a long time before she was completely sure. But eventually, she found what she was looking for.

One day she saw Bart working in the warehouse. She approached him and said, "What happened to the last map we found?"

Bart shrugged gloomily. "Who cares? We can't use it anyway."

"I think we can," Elli said.

"Olana and I already tried talking to Tylee," Bart said. "We about got in a fistfight. Tylee just won't back down. No more excavs. Period."

Elli could feel her pulse thrumming in her ears. She couldn't believe what she was about to say. But she managed to stammer out what she'd been thinking for weeks. "So we go anyway," she said.

Bart's eyebrows went up. "What!"

"So we go anyway."

"You're talking about—" He paused, and his voice dropped almost to a whisper. "You're talking about an *unauthorized* excav?"

"Why not?"

Bart looked around nervously. "Look, there are a lot of things that go into an excav," he whispered. "Any one mistake could lead the dados back here. And then all our work would be for nothing. I supervise the dig. Olana organizes the excav—the timing, the location, and all that stuff. And the driver—well, he works directly for Tylee. We break everything up like this so that if Blok security ever captures somebody, they can't give up all our secrets."

"Yes, but—"

"Only Tylee and three drivers know the location of this warehouse. Even Olana and I enter and leave wearing blindfolds. Without one of Tylee's drivers, we could never find our way back here."

Elli took a deep breath. "I'm not so sure of that."

"The drivers are absolutely loyal to Tylee."

"We don't need them."

Bart narrowed his eyes. "You know someone who can get us in and out of here?"

Elli nodded.

"Who?" Bart demanded.

Elli's voice was so soft, she could barely be heard.

"Me," she whispered.

Ten

When Elli had been swept into the warehouse after the pit collapsed several years earlier, the wall had been quickly rebuilt. But after she started living in her broom closet, she noticed that the air in the closet had a different smell from the rest of the warehouse. It was an earthy, oily smell. Not bad—just different.

And it came through a vent in the ceiling.

After a while it occurred to her that the air was coming from the tunnel she had been propelled through by the mud.

She pretty much forgot about it—until the idea popped into her mind of doing the unauthorized excav. If she could get to the tunnel . . . well, the tunnel must lead *somewhere*. Right?

So she had looked at the old maps of the city and found what it had to be. Many years earlier the city had had a subway. Eventually the subway had been shut down and sealed up. But the tunnels were still there. There had to be a way to get in and out of them.

Elli felt the strongest compulsion she'd ever felt in her life. She had to go on this excav. She *had* to.

One night, after all the workers at Mr. Pop had left, she crawled up through the vent. As she shinnied on her belly through the narrow concrete shaft, she giggled to herself. *Imagine me, a little gray-haired cleaning lady, sneaking through an air shaft like some hero in a movie!*

She didn't really even feel scared. It was an adventure!

After only twenty or thirty feet, she ran into a grimy old metal grate. She shined her flashlight through it. On the other side was a dark, tiled tunnel. She pushed the grate open, slid onto the dirty floor and looked around. On the floor below her, half buried in mud and debris, were rusting old tracks leading off into the distance.

Yes! This might work!

She began walking. Within an hour, she had found what she needed.

On the day of the excav, the team members had furtively slipped into Elli's little broom closet.

Then Elli had led them through the ventilation duct, and through a maze of underground tunnels. Eventually they looked up and saw a thin beam of light coming from a tiny hole at the top of a very long, dark shaft. A rusty iron ladder led to the top.

"We'll climb to the top," she said. "At the top you'll put your blindfolds on. Olana has arranged for a driver to pull a van up next to a certain manhole. The driver doesn't know where we've come from, who we are, or what our mission is. He'll be there at exactly ten seventeen a.m. The traffic light will turn red, and he'll stop. We'll have eight seconds to get into the van. I'll lead you out of the shaft and into the van. Don't make a move without me. Clear?"

The other members of the team looked at one another wonderingly. They had never seen this side of Elli Winter. She had always been a nice, quiet middle-aged lady who had an odd knack for finding buried boxes.

"You're a woman of many surprises," one of the diggers said. He poked her teasingly in the forehead. "What else have you got hidden in that head of yours?"

Elli felt a flush of pleasure. It was silly, this strapping young boy making a fuss over her. But still, it was nice.

She looked at the watch she had borrowed from Olana. "Let's go," she said.

Three hours later they were digging. It was an idyllic spot. Small forested mountains rose from each side of a flat, meadowed valley. In the middle of the valley, a small river babbled over smooth black rocks. It was spring, so the grass was full of beautiful yellow flowers that stretched off as far as the eye could see.

But the ground where they were digging was a hard-packed clay, full of rocks. It was miserable work, slower than Elli had hoped.

The necklace around her neck felt hotter here than it had ever felt. Something important was buried in this ground. Elli felt more sure of it than anything she'd ever felt in her life. But the hole was getting deeper and deeper. And they still hadn't found anything.

Finally Olana said, "This is one of the deepest holes

we've ever dug. Are you sure it's in the right place?"

"As sure as I *can* be, dear," Elli said.

"I'm getting nervous," Olana said. "This is taking too long. And we don't have any watchers to give us advance warning."

As if on cue, Elli's shovel struck something. It made a thump, rather than the clang of shovel on rock.

"We're there," Bart said.

They began to dig furiously. Elli could see that this was not a normal box. Usually the boxes were made of metal. This was made of some kind of unusual plastic.

"Five more minutes and we'll have it," Bart said.

Then Elli heard something that made her skin crawl. A sudden intake of breath.

"Oh, no," Olana whispered. Then a louder shout. "Run!"

"Go!" Bart said. He interlaced his fingers, so that the two younger diggers could plant their feet on his hands and climb out. They were gone in seconds. "Come on!" he said to Elli.

"You next," she said. "You're taller. You can pull me out."

Bart didn't have to be asked twice. Elli simply bent over at the waist, and he used her back as a step, bounding out of the hole. Then he reached back in.

Elli looked up at him for a moment. She could hear the swoosh of the helicopter blades now. She wanted to go. In fact, she was completely terrified. She knew that the dados would be there very soon. But at the same time, she had to keep digging. She had no choice. Elli shook her head at Bart.

"Run, dear," she said softly.

"Are you crazy?" Bart shouted.

"I have to keep digging. Go."

"Run!" somebody shouted again.

Bart looked at her incredulously. She turned away and began digging. She heard pounding footsteps as Bart sprinted away toward the tree line.

She could hear the chopper getting closer, the whine of its engine piercing as a dental drill. She had never been more scared in her life. But she kept digging.

All this time she had been feeling drawn to come here and dig. But she'd never really thought about what was in the box. Something important—important to the movement, important to the revivers, important to Mr. Pop.

But now the security dados would have it. They'd take it back to some faceless building owned by Blok. There would be a brief review by some sour little man. And then a dado would take it to some dirty furnace and burn it. Whatever *it* was.

She managed to get the shovel under the lip of the box. Tilting the shovel handle back, she forced the box up, free of the hard clay. *At least let me see it,* she thought.

She snuck a glance over her shoulder. The security chopper was racing up the valley, its belly swaying back and forth as the aircraft tracked the gentle bends in the river.

Maybe there was time. With a herculean effort, she hoisted the box out, tossed it over the lip of the hole. Then she used the shovel to propel herself up onto the grass.

The chopper was hovering above her now. She looked up, but could see no faces, no signs of human life. And in fact, she knew, there was no human life up there. Just dados—mindless machines, intent on their mission.

The downdraft from the chopper blades whipped at her hair and clothes. The air was full of yellow flowers, ripped from the ground by the prop wash.

She bent over the box, flipped the lid open.

Above her, she heard a loud noise, like zippers being opened. As she looked up, she saw what it was—the sound of the dados sliding down long black ropes that hung from the belly of the aircraft.

Four dados slid toward the ground. All of them tall, hard faced, bulky. All of them armed with gold stun guns. Their faces showed no mercy.

"Lie down, citizen!" one of them shouted. "Lie down and lace your fingers behind your head."

For a moment Elli thought, *Well, maybe I should. It's all over now anyway, right?*

But instead, she reached into the box.

ELEVEN

From the top of the hill, Olana watched through the binoculars.

"What a shame," Bart said. "I guess that's the end of the road for the cleaning lady, huh?"

Through her fieldglasses Olana saw the small gray-haired woman reach into the box. Then she stood up. There was something in her hands—an odd-looking stick that glinted silver in the bright sun.

The security dados were moving slowly toward her, forming a loose circle around her. They had not even drawn their stunners. Four dados against one small middle-aged woman—it was no contest.

"What's that in her hand?" Bart said.

"I'm trying to—" Olana broke off. The surprise of what happened next was so great that she was speechless.

As the first dado approached, Elli lunged suddenly. Olana's eyes widened. The odd silver stick simply passed into the dado's chest, as though it were made of butter.

The dado crumpled—a puppet with its strings cut.

For a moment no one moved. Olana was barely able to make out the expression on Elli's face. The little woman looked shocked. The dados too were clearly taken by surprise. Whatever the silver stick was, it was not like any weapon they had encountered before. They weren't programmed to respond to it.

Apparently, Elli's moment of shock passed quickly. She immediately started chopping through the air with the silver stick, waving it wildly around her. It passed straight through the neck of the next dado. The second dado too went down. It hit the ground and didn't move.

These dados were top-of-the-line combat models. They were built to adjust to changing circumstances. They clawed for their stunners.

One of the dados fired, missing narrowly. Elli dodged, brought her stick down on his arm. The hand flew off, still clutching its stunner. Before the dado's limp body could fall, though, the little woman had grabbed it. Using the body as a shield, she staggered forward, the downed dado absorbing shot after shot from the last dado's stunner.

Realizing that it wouldn't be able to shoot her as long as she was holding its fallen comrade, the surviving dado simply charged at Elli. She chopped at him with her silver stick. But this time he was ready, blocking it with his stunner. Evidently the silver stick could pass through the body of a dado—but not through the metal stunner.

Using his sheer bulk, he slammed Elli backward. The silver stick fell from her arm, bounced, slid into the pit.

"No!" Olana said. "No, no, no!"

"What happened?" Bart said.

Olana lost track of the cleaning lady for a moment as she staggered out of the binoculars' range of view. Then all she could see was a flash of cheap gray material falling into the pit. Elli's coat.

Olana scanned the area looking for a sign of the cleaning lady. She was gone.

"They shot her, I think," Olana said. "She's in the hole now."

The surviving dado cautiously approached the hole, its gold stunner extended. Olana sighed. Well, it was an amazing performance. Elli had offered up her life to give the rest of the team a chance to get away.

"We've got to go," Olana said. "While we've still got a chance."

"Wait," Bart said. "Just wait. Another ten seconds. We owe her that."

Olana lifted the binoculars again. Just in time to see a flash in the bright sunlight.

The silver stick came pushing up out of the hole. The dado tried to dodge—but it was too late. The silver stick sliced right through its chest.

The dado fell like a rag doll.

Olana stared.

"What?" Bart said, straining to see what had just happened.

"She did it!" Olana said wonderingly. "She—"

But it wasn't over. The small woman clambered out of the hole. The dados were all down, but the chopper was still functioning. It had landed a short distance from the hole. When the fourth dado fell, its engine began spooling up as though it were getting ready to take off.

"Look out!" Olana shouted. "The chopper! Get the chopper!"

But Elli couldn't hear. The sound of the chopper drowned out her voice. Olana wondered if she saw the gold stunner protruding from the nose of the chopper. It wasn't aimed at her. But if the chopper got airborne, it could swing the stunner around at her.

"Elli! Run!"

Apparently, Elli noticed the threat at the same time as Olana. But instead of running away, she ran *toward* the chopper.

Elli reached the aircraft just as its wheels cleared the ground, and she jumped awkwardly, just barely landing on the craft. *What was she doing?*

The chopper bounced, then lifted up. Slowly the aircraft gained speed and began to scud across the ground. Suddenly a dark shape flew from the door.

It took Olana a moment to identify the dark shape. It was Elli. The little woman fell for what seemed an eternity—though it was probably only a fraction of a second. Olana screamed as Elli hit the ground hard, then lay motionless.

The chopper slowed, then turned. In horror Olana realized the big gold stunner was now swinging around toward her and the others in the group. The chopper kept turning and turning. The gun grew closer and closer.

"Down! Everybody down!" Olana commanded.

Finally the stunner was aimed directly at them. Olana waited for the blast. But nothing happened. Nothing, that is, except for an odd little wisp of smoke that began to trail from the side of the chopper. The chopper kept wheeling and wheeling, the stunner aiming farther and farther from Olana and her group. *Something is wrong with the chopper!* Olana realized. Elli had done something to the chopper!

Suddenly the chopper dipped, nosed over, and slammed into the mountain, obliterating itself.

"She did it," Olana whispered. Then she shouted it. "She *did* it! She took 'em out!"

A ragged cheer rose from the excav team. They began to stream down the hill toward where Elli lay.

As they grew closer, Olana's heart began to sink. Elli wasn't moving. She wasn't moving at all.

TWELVE

Elli lay on her back. Every part of her body hurt as she stared up at the circle of faces. She felt confused.

"What just happened?" she said.

One of the young diggers grinned at her. "You were incredible! That's what happened!"

Olana picked up a long cylinder. "What *is* this?"

Elli sat up, looked at the gleaming stick for a moment. It started coming back to her, her whole fight with the dados. It seemed almost like a dream, like something that had happened to someone else. Because Elli knew that she was not the fight-off-hordes-of-dados kind of person.

Elli blinked, took a deep breath, then took the cylinder from Olana, put it back in the box, and slammed the lid. "We need to get back to the warehouse right now," she said. "The chopper will have sent out some kind of distress signal. More dados will come."

She stood, tucked the box under her arm, and began trotting toward their vehicle.

~

The trip home was silent. Several times dado choppers buzzed over, heading rapidly in the direction of the downed aircraft. But no one stopped them.

They descended into the manhole and within fifteen minutes they were crawling through the air duct into Elli's little broom closet.

They emerged from the broom closet to find a ring of people standing outside the door. Their faces were hard and angry. Standing at the center of the group was Tylee.

"You did an excav against my *express* orders!" she shouted. "What are you people thinking? Dados could be on the way here right this minute!"

"Look," Elli said, "it's all my fault. You see, I—"

Tylee cut her off. "If it was just some little cleaning lady, I'd be more understanding. But Olana? Bart? You two are supposed to be leaders. Responsible! Intelligent!"

Bart and Olana were ashen faced. "I'm sorry, but—," Olana began.

"You've endangered *everything*. Everything we've worked for! Everything we've bled for! Everything we've—"

This time it was Elli's turn to cut Tylee off.

"Dear," Elli said. Her voice was soft. But it felt surprisingly firm coming out. "Dear, this was our final excav. We understand that it was a risk. But this was a risk worth taking."

"You are in *no* position to evaluate what is or is not a reasonable risk. There are matters at stake here that—"

Elli smiled shyly. "I'm sorry, dear, but I think you'll

see that what's in this box was worth the risk." She set the long thin dirty box on a nearby table. "See for yourself."

Tylee opened the box grudgingly, pulled out the long gleaming cylinder. She frowned at it skeptically. "What is this—a shower-curtain rod? A piece of an old vehicle?" She tossed it back on the table.

Bart stepped forward, picked up the cylinder. "It's a weapon. Tylee, this little cleaning woman—as you call her—used this thing to destroy four dados and a security chopper. In about thirty seconds."

Tylee looked at the weapon, then at Elli, then at the weapon again.

"Is this true?" she finally said to Elli.

Elli nodded.

"That 'curtain rod,'" Olana said, "is our hope for the future."

There was a sudden hubbub as everyone started talking. Olana began excitedly giving a blow-by-blow description of Elli's fight with the dados. And all of the revivers began grabbing for the cylinder, anxious to figure out what its secret was.

Elli let them talk, feeling a pleased sensation moving through her entire body. During the excav, she had felt a nervous buzzing at the back of her skull. *What if I fail? What if I take a wrong turn? What if the dados catch us? What if Blok tracks us back to the warehouse? What if . . .* But now she knew that her faith had been repaid.

Finally she interrupted the clamoring voices. "Excuse me," she said. "Excuse me."

Everyone quieted, then turned to look at her.

"Yes?" Tylee said.

"When I said that what was in the box was worth the risk, I was actually talking about the *other* item in the box."

Tylee frowned curiously, then and reached into the box a second time.

"What is it?" Bart said.

Tylee pulled out a book—a very old leather-bound volume. Her eyes widened. Then she held up the book so everyone could see. On the cover were four words, set in faded gold type:

The Analects of Kelln.

There was a long moment of silence.

Olana spoke first. "Wow."

"Oh, my," said another voice.

"You *found* it," Tylee whispered. "I'd like you to give it to Dr. Pender in person." Then she handed the book to Elli.

The group turned away and started talking about the weapon again. Elli hugged the precious book to her chest. It smelled of ancient libraries.

I did it! she thought. *I found the* Analects of Kelln! It occurred to her—as it had every now and then—that maybe there was something to what Press had told her. Maybe she really was . . .

No. No, it was silly to even consider it. She was a cleaning lady. Maybe she had an odd gift for finding important old boxes. Maybe, with the help of the strange cylinder and about a ton of adrenaline, she had been able to fight off a couple of brainless robots. But that didn't mean she was a Traveler. That didn't mean she was special.

She left the group and began walking toward Dr. Pender's office. The excited voices faded.

Elli found Dr. Pender standing in his office. He looked up, raised one eyebrow, and said, "You caused a bit of a fuss today. I must say, I really don't understand why you would have done such a thing."

Wordlessly, she handed him the book. He smiled tightly as he took the volume. She could tell that, like Tylee, he was angry that anyone would engage in an unauthorized excav. He was understandably protective of the warehouse and its irreplaceable contents.

But then Dr. Pender's face changed. His mouth opened slightly as he stared at the cover of the volume. He opened it reverently and began to leaf through the pages. After a moment, tears began streaming down his face. Finally the librarian looked up at her with an odd smile on his face.

"You did it. . . .," he whispered. "How did you know? How did you—" His voice faltered.

She shrugged. *I just knew*, she thought. *I just did.*

Solemnly he closed the book. Then he held it out to her. "You must be the first one to read it," he said.

"Oh, I couldn't, dear," she said. "Someone who understands these things better should—"

He pressed his finger against her lip. "Shhh."

"But—"

"I've heard you whispering while you work," he said. "Quoting the books you've read."

Elli blushed. She felt embarrassed to think that anybody had noticed her. She had thought it was her little secret.

"You're memorizing them all." Dr. Pender stared at her intently. "Aren't you?"

She looked at the floor. "I suppose I am."

He pushed the book into her hands. "One day the dados may come," he said. "Perhaps even today. Who knows. So it's important that you put this in here." He tapped the side of her head. "The sooner the better."

She nodded and began walking back toward her broom closet. She wanted to store the book on her special shelf.

When she reached the broom closet, Tylee was there waiting for her. "Ah!" she said. "There you are."

"I know you're mad," Elli said. "I'm sorry. I should have—"

"Don't even think about it," Tylee said. "What's done is done."

The leader of the revivers stood there awkwardly for a moment. "Do you mind if I speak with you privately?"

Elli nodded. "Come in," she said, opening the door to the tiny broom closet. "I'm afraid you'll have to sit on the bed," she added.

Tylee looked around the tiny room. "You *live* in here?" She shook her head. "I never knew. I thought you had a real room. I'm sorry. We should have—"

Elli smiled gently. "I like it here."

Tylee spotted the photographs cut from newspapers that covered the walls. Nevva winning prizes. Nevva holding up trophies. Nevva smiling at the camera. "Your daughter," she said.

Elli nodded.

"You've never told anyone here your real name."

Elli nodded.

"We had to find out of course. It was in the papers, a woman missing the day of the cave-in. We pulled up the records and identified you from the photographs. We had to be careful in case you were a Blok spy."

Elli sat on the bed with her hands between her knees. "Of course."

Tylee sighed, her face etched with worry. "We're going to have to move Mr. Pop," she said. "We've been thinking about it for a while. A site farther out in the country. After what happened on your excav . . . well, we suspect that Blok has a general idea of where we're located. After what you did out there today, they'll leave no stone unturned trying to find this place."

"I'm sorry," Elli said. "I know that we attracted too much attention with this last excav."

"Don't apologize. It was worth it." Tylee hesitated, as though she were trying to find the right words. "In fact, today may well be the turning point in our movement. That cylinder, whatever it is—our scientists will try to figure out how it works. If we can reproduce it, make more, we can finally rise up and destroy Blok."

Elli nodded.

"But something else happened today. Something I can tell only you. But first you must promise never to speak of this again."

"Okay."

"We recruited a new agent today. This person will be the most important, most highly placed agent our movement has ever recruited."

"Oh?"

"With the new agent? And that weapon you found? We *will* triumph."

Elli didn't speak. *Why is Tylee speaking to me*

about this? she thought. A highly placed agent of the movement—that's something that a person like Tylee wouldn't talk about. The more people you told a thing like that, the more chance of the information leaking to Blok security.

"The agent's name . . ." Tylee paused. "Elli, it's Nevva Winter. Our new agent is your daughter."

Elli took a deep breath.

"I just thought you should know."

Tylee rose and left the broom closet.

Elli sat on the bed for a long time. After the day she'd just had, she was exhausted. And the fight with the dados—the effect of it was just catching up with her. She began trembling.

I should get to work, she thought. *I should go clean something.* But her legs were trembling so hard, she couldn't even stand up.

And then, as quickly as it had hit her, the feeling passed.

You know what? she thought. *I've cleaned every single day for the past five years. Who's to say I can't take a day off?*

She felt a strong glow spreading through her limbs. She was exhausted. But she was triumphant, too. In a funny sort of way, she felt better than she'd felt . . . well, before her husband had begun the long slide that led her to this tiny room.

With that, she picked up the book and began to read *The Analects of Kelln*. As she read the first sentence, a strange smile spread across her face. And like Dr.

Pender, tears of joy began to run down her face.

Even at the end of the road, read the first sentence, *there is a road. Even at the end of the road, a new road stretches out, limitless and open, a road that may lead anywhere. To him who will find it, there is always a road.*

ALDER

ONE

There was nothing in the world that Alder had wanted more than to become a full-fledged Bedoowan knight. A Bedoowan knight was strong. A Bedoowan knight was just. A Bedoowan knight was brave. A Bedoowan knight was a hero to all people, respected by all.

And now Alder was a knight. In fact, he was generally known as the finest of all knights. When Alder's name was spoken, it summoned up everything that was virtuous in a Bedoowan knight.

On this particular day he was riding through the dark, forbidding forest of Arlberg on his powerful black warhorse. As he rode, he heard a sudden scream of anguish pierce the gloom. He wheeled the horse around and spurred it toward the cry.

In seconds he had reached the source of the sound. A beautiful young villager, obviously caught in the middle of doing her washing, was surrounded by highwaymen—the unscrupulous robbers who lived deep in the forest, preying on travelers.

"Please!" she cried. "Someone help me!"

"Unhand her, you cowards!" Alder shouted. The high-waymen whirled fearfully.

Alder drew his sword, brandishing it high, as his horse reared up in the middle of the stream. Then he charged. Seeing him, the highwaymen scattered like leaves in the wind.

All of them, that is, except for their leader—a tall, muscular man with a scar running down his face. He grabbed the beautiful young villager, putting a thin, rusted blade to her neck. "Come and get me, knight," the man shouted.

Alder swung his sword and—

"Alder!"

Alder swung his sword and galloped toward—

"Alder!"

Alder swung his sword and galloped toward the— toward—galloped toward the—

"Hey, Alder! Snap out of the daydream, you nitwit!" Master Horto, the head of the Imperial Training Academy, was yelling at Alder. As usual. "I'm not telling you again! Get me some water. And while you're at it, a couple of those pastries. The ones with the jelly inside."

It took a moment for Alder's mind to adjust. He was standing in the rear of the academy's training hall, while Master Horto led the sword class. The students—knights in training—were all lined up and repeating their sword drills. All except Alder.

Alder wasn't permitted to train with the others. He had other duties.

Alder ran into the other room, came back with some

water and the tray of pastries. Master Horto was a huge man—even taller than Alder, and weighing about as much as two ordinary men.

"Here you are, Master." Alder bowed and held out the water and the tray of pastries.

Horto grabbed one of the pastries, stuffed the entire thing in his mouth. As he chewed, a disgusted expression ran across his face. He spit the entire pastry on the training floor. "That one's old! Did you just give me *yesterday's* pastries?"

"Well, I just—"

Master Horto cuffed him across the head so hard his ears rang. "Clean that up." He pointed at the floor.

The other trainees tittered and pointed as Alder knelt and began cleaning the floor with a rag. Alder sighed and smiled, trying to pretend it didn't bother him to be laughed at. But it did bother him. It always did. He had been the butt of jokes every single day since he joined the academy three years ago.

Joined? Well, officially he was a trainee. But he never trained with the other students. Master Horto had him so busy cleaning and fetching and doing other menial jobs around the school that he never had time to train.

"As soon as you get your chores done, you can train," Master Horto would always say.

Only . . . the chores never got done. No matter how hard Alder worked. Now he was sixteen years old, and he still knew next to nothing about fighting.

Alder's problem was that he was an orphan. He had no parents, no friends, no supporters, no patrons, no money. And since he couldn't pay fees to the academy, Master

Horto required him to work. And work. And work.

Most of the boys at the academy would have their knighthoods within a year. But Alder? Knighthood seemed very far away. In fact, if he didn't get on with his training soon, he was going to be in serious trouble.

There were actually a few Bedoowans who never became knights. Usually they were people who had physical or mental problems that kept them from completing their training. Poor, pathetic wretches who shambled around the castle with long faces, avoiding people's eyes, constantly abused by everyone. They were called every horrible name in the book—"cripples," "weaklings," "half-wits." They were laughed at and despised even by the Novans, the people who worked as servants to the Bedoowans, and by the Milago, the people who worked the glaze mines in the village below the castle.

The thought that Alder might end up wandering around the castle without any respect, without any status at all—the very thought of it made him sick to his stomach. But what could he do? If Master Horto wouldn't let him train . . .

The thing was, if you didn't make your knighthood by age eighteen, you were out of the running. Alder only had two years. And two years was a very short time to learn all the skills a knight was supposed to know.

You had to be a decent horseman, a passable archer, proficient with pike and glaive and short spear. And of course, most of all, you had to be an excellent swordsman. If you couldn't show real skill with a sword, you were sunk.

Alder practiced secretly in his tiny room, memorizing

moves from the academy curriculum and then practicing them until late into the night. But that wasn't the same as practicing at school.

"Class dismissed," Horto shouted.

The trainee knights, laughing and joking, began packing up their equipment.

Alder started packing up his equipment too. He was never allowed to use it, but he brought it anyway. One of these days he was going to be allowed to train. And when that day came, he'd be ready.

"Alder!" Master Horto stood over Alder, his fists on his hips. "Where do you think *you're* going?"

"Sir, uh, Master, I have guard duty tonight at the north gate of the castle, so, uh, I was thinking—" Alder ducked his head respectfully.

Master Horto glared at him through narrowed eyes. "You were *thinking* were you? Thinking?"

"Well, Master, I—"

"Don't *think*. Do what you're told. Get that floor cleaned up. Then get to your post!"

Two

It was well past supper by the time Alder arrived at his post. He was late because Horto had kept him busy with chores. He'd had no time to eat. Eman and Neman, two boys Alder knew from the academy, were standing at the gate in their armor.

"You're late, you big flabby goof!" Eman said. Eman and Neman took every chance they got to torture Alder. They were actually younger than he was. But they had been knighted just months ago, and so they outranked him.

"We're gonna take a break," Neman said. "Don't move a muscle!"

"But . . ." Alder cleared his throat. "We're supposed to have no fewer than three guards at the gate at any time. Our orders are—"

"Who's the senior guard here, huh?" Eman said.

"Uh . . ."

"Yeah. Thought so," Neman said. "I don't know if you noticed, Alder, but nobody comes to this gate at night. So shut your piehole and do what you're told." He and Eman turned and wandered into the guardhouse, snickering.

"Okay, okay."

"*Excuse* me, trainee?" Neman said, eyes wide.

"I mean, uh—yes, sir."

"That's better." Neman whirled and walked away.

It galled Alder to call the two younger boys "sir." But what could he do about it? Rules were rules. So Alder stood there like a lump, getting colder and colder and colder. And hungrier and hungrier and hungrier.

After a while the tantalizing smell of roast mutton and fresh bread began wafting out of the guardhouse. His stomach rumbled. Finally he couldn't stand it anymore. He looked around to make sure nobody was approaching the gate, then ran quickly to the guardhouse.

He found Eman and Neman eating. There was a big fire in the fireplace.

"What are you doing?" Eman said, smacking his lips. "Go back to your post!"

"Don't I get to eat sometime?" Alder said.

Neman snorted.

"Anyway . . . I thought you guys were coming right back. What if somebody comes?"

Eman looked up, a piece of meat sticking out of his mouth, gravy on his chin. "Show 'em who's boss," he said. Then he winked slyly at Neman.

Eman turned his back and grabbed a pigeon wing from the pile of hot food. Alder's stomach rumbled. "Could I just—"

"Are you still here?" Neman said. "Get back to your post. And don't bother us again!"

Alder went back out and stood there with his pike, shifting from foot to foot. The moon went behind a cloud. It was starting to get kind of spooky.

Hours passed. Eman and Neman were nowhere to be seen. He knew the captain of the guards would make a tour around midnight. Eman and Neman would kill him if they got caught away from their post. They'd be sure to make it out to be his fault somehow.

Finally he decided he'd better check on them. He ran back to the guardhouse. Eman and Neman were snoozing away on the floor by the fire. Every scrap of food was gone. Alder was in a bind. They'd get mad if he woke them. The captain of the guard probably wouldn't be there for another half hour. Better to let them sleep. They might wake up on their own.

Alder walked quickly back to the gate. He was surprised to see a small man approaching the castle from out of the darkness.

The man was quite old and shabbily dressed, and he leaned on a gnarled cane. His body was concealed by a threadbare cloak. His face was very thin, as though every bit of fat had been chiseled from his skull. A poor farmer, Alder guessed. Though it was certainly unusual for farmers to approach the castle at this time of night. And market day wasn't until Friday.

"Why weren't you at your post?" the old man snapped, pointing his gnarled cane at Alder's chest.

"Excuse me?" Alder said.

The old man looked around irritably. In the light of the flickering torch, the old man's eyes glittered strangely. "There should be at least four of you guarding the gate."

Alder decided he'd better take control of the situation. This old farmer didn't seem to understand the correct tone for speaking to a Bedoowan knight. Even if Alder wasn't a full-fledged knight, he was a guard at King Karel's castle. Respect was due. "Um . . . state your business, old man."

"My business is *my* business," the old man said. There was something in his eyes, an intensity, that seemed unlike a farmer. Alder wondered if maybe the old man were crazy.

"Right . . . well . . . I need you to state your business. Otherwise I can't admit you."

"Oh, really?" the old man said.

"Eman!" Alder called. He had a feeling this old man was going to cause trouble. Alder didn't know quite what he should do. "Neman!"

"That's it," the old man said. "Call for reinforcements."

"I'm just a trainee," Alder said apologetically. Then he felt foolish. He was letting this old farmer get under his skin.

"A *trainee*? At *your* age?" The old man sounded appalled. "I'd be ashamed to be a trainee at your age."

Alder blushed. He *was* ashamed to be a trainee. He felt like saying he was a victim of circumstance, giving him the I'm-just-a-poor-orphan speech that he used to justify all his shortcomings. But he figured the old farmer would just make fun of him even more.

Eman and Neman showed up out of breath, buckling on their armor. "What!" Eman demanded. "What's going on?"

"Sorry to bother you. But this old man wants admittance," Alder said.

Eman looked the ragged old man up and down. "You woke us up for *this*, Alder?" he said.

Neman poked at the old man with his pike. "What do you mean by disturbing Bedoowan knights at this time of night?"

The old man placed one finger on the pike, redirecting it just enough to avoid getting poked in the ribs with its sharp point. "You're a very rude young man," the old man said. "Has anybody ever told you that?"

Eman and Neman looked at each other. "Did he just say what I think he did?" Neman said.

"I believe he did, Neman," Eman said.

Eman's eyes narrowed as he turned back to the old man. "Who do you think you are?"

"Deserting your post?" the old man said. "Leaving the safety and security of the castle in the hands of a chubby, over-aged trainee? I'm not at all impressed with you two."

Eman and Neman had had enough. Neman lifted his pike and brought it down hard, obviously intending to whack the old man in the head with its wooden shaft.

But the old man deftly parried the blow with his goofy-looking cane, and then whacked Neman in the shin with it.

"Ow!" Neman said, dropping his pike and clutching at his leg. "Owwwwww! I think you broke my leg."

"All right, that's *it*!" Eman said. He jabbed his pike at the old man.

But by the time the pike reached the old man, he was

somewhere else. The sharp spear point passed by him. Eman grunted angrily. Three times he jabbed at the old man, each time, missing by a hair.

"Come on, Alder!" Eman shouted finally. "Help me out!"

Alder leaned his pike against the wall and drew his sword. "Ah!" the old man said. "Now someone's showing some common sense. Pikes are worthless for individual combat. They're intended for engaging mounted cavalry. Didn't anyone ever teach you that? If you want to fight a man on foot, use a sword!"

"What do you know about fighting, you stupid old farmer?" Eman said. But as he spoke, he hurled his pike down and drew his sword.

Alder held back and let Eman press the attack. He had no confidence that he'd be of much use in a sword fight anyway. After all, he hadn't had even a shred of training, had he?

The old man parried nimbly as the younger, larger man attacked him. Chunks of wood flew out of his stick as Eman whaled away at him. But the old man didn't look the slightest bit afraid. In fact, his face was as impassive as a mask. Finally Eman chopped his stick in half. The old man stood with the stump in his hand.

"Seems I have you at a disadvantage, old man," Eman said, pointing his blade toward the old man's throat.

"In what sense?" the old man said. Then he threw back his cloak. Visible for the first time, were the old man's clothes. He was dressed like a Bedoowan, not a farmer. And hanging from his wide leather belt was a sword. The handle was not ornate, but it had the look of a well-used tool—polished to a soft gleam, as though by regular practice.

"Who are you?" Eman said nervously.

"You know, you might have been wise to ask that earlier," the old man said. Then he began to attack Eman. Not with the sword, though—to Alder's amazement—but with the hacked off piece of wood in his hand. And though Eman defended himself, he seemed powerless to keep the old man from driving him backward.

"Help me!" Eman shouted. "Neman, do something! Sound the alarm!"

But Neman was still rolling on the ground, moaning and holding his leg.

With that the old man tripped Eman, stripping his sword with one hand and pressing the sharp point of the wooden stick to Eman's throat with the other. Eman froze. The old man turned to Alder. "So, young trainee, are you going to admit me to the castle? Or are you going to fight me?"

"Uh . . ."

"Wrong answer, dear boy!" The old man hurled Eman's sword at Alder. It passed between his legs, piercing his cloak and sinking its point deep into the door behind him, pinning him to the wall.

The old man sighed and shook his head disgustedly. "Pathetic," he said. "Pathetic, miserable, appalling, nauseating performance."

Then he walked past them.

"If you wish to arrest me," he called over his shoulder, "you may find me at the Seven Arms Inn. Tell them to ask the innkeeper for Wencil of Peldar."

"I guess I better go get the captain of the guards, huh?" Alder said weakly after the old man had disappeared.

Eman leaped to his feet, ran over to Alder, and whacked him in the head. "If you even *think* of telling anybody about what just happened here, I'll skin you alive."

"All right, yes."

"Yes, *what*?"

"Yes, *sir*."

Eman looked at Neman and shook his head sadly, as if to say, *Will he never learn?*

THREE

Three days later Alder was trudging up the High Street toward the academy when he noticed a small sign hanging over the window of a building that had been empty for quite a few years. It read:

WENCIL OF PELDAR
MASTER OF ARMS
INSTRUCTION OFFERED TO YOUNG
BEDOOWAN GENTLEMEN
INQUIRE WITHIN

Alder stood rooted to the ground, looking at the sign. The building was much like Wencil himself—shabby. One of the windows was broken out. The walls needed painting. The roof looked like it needed to be rethatched. Alder held his sword and the various wooden practice weapons in his hand. It seemed ridiculous, carrying the weapons around with him all the time. Every day he carried them from his little room in the castle to the academy—as though he were actually going to *use* them. And every day he did nothing but sweep the academy and cut wood and carry things around for Master Horto's obnoxious wife.

He studied the sign some more. Master of arms. That meant that the old man taught the knightly arts—swordsmanship and so on. For years Master Horto had been the only certified master of arms in the castle.

Wencil of Peldar was a nobody, of course. He was no Master Horto. If you wanted to be a knight, you obviously had to train with Horto, a man with a reputation at court. Still, Alder was intrigued by the sign. He wondered idly if there were some way he could at least pick up a few tips from the old man.

Out of curiosity as much as anything, Alder tentatively pushed open the front door of the building. It groaned on rusty hinges. He found himself in a very small, cold, empty room.

"Hello?" he said.

There was no answer.

"Hello?"

He walked tentatively into the next room. It too was empty. And yet . . . He felt the hairs come up on the back of his neck. *Someone is here!* He was sure of it.

He quietly leaned his practice weapons against the wall—all of them except his wooden sword. He gripped the sword tightly and crossed the room as silently as he could. "Hello?" he whispered. "Sir? Master Wencil?"

He thought he heard something in the next room. A squeak? A slight exhalation of breath? He wasn't sure.

He moved as silently as he could into the next room. *Whack!*

For a moment Alder didn't know what had happened. He whirled around as pain shot through his shoulders. Standing behind him was Wencil. How in the world had he gotten there? In Wencil's hand was a stick, much like the one he'd carried the first time Alder met him.

"Sneak into my home, would you?" the old man shouted.

"But I—the sign said—I was just—"

"Defend yourself or die!" the old man shouted. Then he began attacking Alder with the stick. Alder desperately tried to defend himself. But it was pointless. The old man, grinning broadly, drove him backward.

Whack! Whack! Whack!

The stick caught him on his shin, his elbow, his arm—flicking out like the tongue of a snake. By the time Alder got his sword anywhere near the stick, it was already hitting him someplace else.

"Please! I was just trying to—"

Alder could see he was wasting his effort trying to talk to this man. He decided his best hope was to make for the door.

Whack! Whack! Whack!

Apparently the old man saw what he was trying to do: He bounded in front of Alder, cutting off his escape. Alder tried to make for the back of the building. Surely there would be a door there!

Whack, whack, whack! The stick hit him again and again. And yet, the old man never quite finished him off. After a while Alder started to get the feeling that Wencil was just toying with him. But try as he might, Alder couldn't escape.

Soon Alder was feeling breathless and winded. His legs were like rubber, and his arms could barely hold the sword.

"Keep your guard up!" the old man shouted. "Or I might—" *Whack!* "Be forced—" *Whack!* "To pummel you in the head!" *Whack whack whack!*

Alder felt a sense of gloom and desperation fill him. There was nothing he could do to stop the old man. And he had no strength left.

Then he saw it. His last chance. The old man had driven him into the corner of the room farthest back in the house. It had a broken window through which blew a cold wind.

The window! If he could just get to—

With his last shred of energy, Alder parried the old man's cane, and dove through the window. There was a rush of air and a brief feeling of freedom before . . .

Splat!

Alder sat up. Yuck! He had landed in a large, smelly pile of something.

A bunch of muddy pigs stared at him with angry pink eyes.

Oh, god! He knew what he'd fallen into now. He tried to stand up, slipped, fell again. The smell was awful. And the sticky feeling against his skin. Horrible!

For a moment he just lay there, eyes closed, imagining all the jokes and laughter and jeering that would follow if he showed up at the academy covered in pig poop. There would be ten times as much ridicule as usual. But if he went home to clean up, Master Horto would punish him for being late.

Finally he opened his eyes.

Only to find a man staring down at him. Wencil.

The old man had his hand out, palm up. "Five pieces of silver, please," Wencil said.

Alder sat up. "Huh?"

"Are you deaf, boy? Give me five pieces of silver!" The old man still had his hand out.

"For *what*?" Five pieces of silver was a lot of money. Alder had no idea what the old man was getting at. He was obviously completely insane.

"For your first lesson."

"My what?"

"Your first lesson."

Alder stared at him. Finally he pointed at the building. "In there? That was . . . a *lesson*?"

"Young man, I am an instructor in the arts of fencing, pikesmanship, spear throwing, strategy, tactics, the equestrian arts, archery, grappling, rope climbing, etc. etc. etc. Didn't you read the sign on the door?"

"Yes, but—"

"Then what in the name of creation do you think I was doing in there? Playing patty-cake? Five pieces of silver, please."

"But . . . I'm sorry, sir, I don't have any money."

"Then go to your parents and get some!"

"I'm afraid I don't have any parents. I'm an orphan."

"An *orphan*?" the old man said sharply. Alder noticed that his eyes were an intense green. "No money at all?"

"None, sir."

"Oh," Wencil said. "In that case your instruction will be complimentary. I'll see you tomorrow at nine sharp. Don't be late."

"But . . . sir, I'm a student at the Academy."

"Not anymore, boy. That charlatan Horto has obviously taught you nothing. You fight like a three-year-old girl. Nine o'clock sharp."

Alder blinked. He had never heard anyone speak that way about Master Horto before. "But—"

The old man wrinkled his nose. "And for goodness sake, clean your clothes. I can't have my students wandering around the castle smelling like pig dung!"

With that, the old man whirled around and disappeared.

FOUR

The next day at nine o'clock, Alder appeared at the door of Wencil's house. Wencil was standing next to the door, tapping his fingers impatiently. "Let's go," he said.

"Where?"

"To my academy."

"But I thought *this* was your—"

"You see, boy, that's your problem. You think too much. Close your mouth, listen, do what you're told. That is the way one becomes a warrior."

"So . . . uh . . . should I bring my weapons?"

"You can throw them in a lake for all I care."

The old man began marching down the street, his cane clacking smartly on the cobblestones. Alder didn't see the point of martial arts lessons if you didn't have weapons. So he carried them behind the old man. Besides, he was very proud of all his training gear. He had spent every bit of what little money he had buying the fanciest wooden training weapons available at the academy. They were custom made for him from genuine striped pakka wood by a famous craftsman in another city. He oiled them every night so that they gleamed.

They walked down the High Street, out the north gate, and down the road. Soon they were out in the woods. Wencil was old, but he sure walked fast. Alder was feeling slightly out of breath. Suddenly the old man stopped, clapped his hands, together and turned around.

"Perfect," he said.

"Where are we?" Alder said.

"In my academy, of course," the old man said.

Alder looked around. They were in the middle of a stand of ancient kena trees. Beneath them was a fragrant mat of kena needles. It was a beautiful spot. But he didn't see a building anywhere. "I don't see it," Alder said.

"This is it!" The old man spread his hands.

"But . . ." Alder frowned.

"Let me ask you a question," the old man said. "Do you think battles happen inside academies? Do you think that knights fight on nice clean straw mats?"

"Well. I guess not."

"Then why should they train there?"

Alder had never thought about it that way.

The old man looked around. "Brisk out here, isn't it. Build a fire."

"Okay." Alder looked around. There wasn't much deadfall on the ground to burn. He was going to have to go forage. "Let me go look around for some wood."

"Why go to all that trouble? You could just burn those." He pointed at Alder's collection of beautiful wooden training weapons.

Alder stared. Surely Wencil was joking.

"Hurry up," Wencil said. "Start the fire. I'm freezing."

"But . . . if I burn my training gear, what will I train with?"

"The whole world is a weapon, boy." Wencil tapped his temple with his finger. "A true knight fights with his mind."

Alder hesitated. His beautiful weapons gleamed dully in the mottled light. The striped wood looked deep as a river. How could he *burn* them? He stalled, gathering some tinder and building a little blaze.

"They're a little long for such a small fire," Wencil said. "Break them up first."

Alder had been told a million times that being a Bedoowan knight was all about doing what you were told. So he broke his weapons one by one over his knee and fed them into the fire.

"Ahhhh! That feels great, huh?" Wencil said, warming his hands over the little fire.

Alder said nothing. He couldn't even speak, he was so angry and hurt. These weapons had represented everything to him. His hope. His future. His soul. His very identity. Without weapons, a Bedoowan knight— even a poor, pathetic trainee—was nothing.

When the fire had burned down to embers, the old man pulled a knife from his belt. It's handle was intricately carved from silver, and the blade showed signs of great age. "Go to the riverbank," the old man said. "You will find small trees sticking up out of the water. They are called 'ipo.' Do you know what an ipo tree looks like?"

Alder nodded sullenly. They were a runty little trash

tree that grew in swampy areas along the river.

"Good. Then go and cut one for me. About this long."
Wencil held his arms out about three and a half feet.

Fifteen minutes later Alder came sloshing back with a piece
of ipo wood, his boots full of water. He had been surprised
at how hard the wood was to cut.

Just to spite the old man, Alder had chosen the
knobbiest, ugliest piece of ipo he could find.

Wencil took the gnarled, homely stick from him,
examined it carefully. You'd have thought it was a work
of art the way he squinted and pored over it, fingering
each minute imperfection.

"You chose well," he said finally, handing it back
to Alder. "Now break it over your knee and throw it
in the fire."

Alder wanted to punch the old man in the face. It
had been a huge pain in the neck cutting the wood.
And now he wanted him to break it? If he'd wanted
firewood, he should have just said so. There were
plenty of dead kena branches on the ground between
here and the riverbank.

Alder tried to break the wood over his knee. It bent.
But it wouldn't break. Alder grunted and strained, turning
red in the face and muttering angrily under his breath.

"Come on, are you that weak?" Wencil said. He sat
down on the ground and crossed his feet. "Harder!"

Alder wrestled with the wood. He felt embarrassed
and foolish.

"It won't break!" Alder shouted finally. "It can't
be done."

The old man cocked his head. "All of that firewood over there," Wencil said. "How much did you pay for it?"

It took Alder a moment to realize what he meant by "firewood." The silly old man was talking about Alder's training weapons, so beautifully made and so lovingly maintained. "Close to a hundred pieces of silver," Alder said through gritted teeth.

"And yet you broke them all without any great strain."

Alder flushed. Now he saw what the old man was getting at. This junky, gnarled piece of ipo was stronger than all of those training weapons he'd been so proud of.

"In the old days," Wencil said, "a Bedoowan knight cut his own piece of ipo on the first day of training. It was expected that he would train with that same piece of ipo for eight, ten, twelve years. If, during that entire decade of training, his weapon broke, it was cause for great shame. He'd chosen unwisely." Wencil's lip curled in disgust. "Now we pay *others* to make our weapons."

Alder looked sheepishly at the ground.

"Being a Bedoowan knight is not about appearances, boy. Those were pretty pieces of wood. And they might have lasted a year or two. But in the long run, they wouldn't have served you. To be a Bedoowan knight is to be like this." He held up the gnarled stick. "A Bedoowan knight serves . . . not the king, not your commander, certainly not your own ego. A Bedoowan knight serves the realm. He serves the good of *all* the people in the realm—Bedoowans, Novans, even the despised Milago who toil under the earth to bring out glaze."

Alder frowned. "But at the academy they say, 'Novans bow, Milagos serve, Bedoowans rule.'"

"To be a Bedoowan is to be responsible. At all times. Not just for yourself, but for those whom you protect. To wear this"—he pulled back his cloak, revealing the hilt of his sword—"to wear *this* is to bear a great responsibility. You hold the power of life and death in your hand. It's not for the faint of heart."

"I try hard to do what I'm told."

"Of course. A Bedoowan must do as he's told." The old man smiled craftily. "Except when he doesn't."

"But . . . how do you know when not to do what you're told?"

The old man patted one wrinkled old hand over his heart. "You always *know*," he said. "The question is whether you take responsibility for what is right. Or whether you don't."

FIVE

For the next six months Alder trained day in and day out. Wencil never took on any more students. He simply led Alder into the forest and trained him from dawn till dark. There were no chores, no sweeping, no cooking, no fetching things. Just train, train, train.

At first Alder suspected that Wencil was a fraud or just crazy. Whenever he ran into anybody from the academy, that's exactly what they said about Wencil. He was a quack, a liar, a lunatic, a has-been, a never-was. Some said he wasn't even a Bedoowan. They had no shortage of insults. Everyone knew Master Horto was the only teacher qualified to instruct anyone in the deepest secrets of Bedoowan knighthood.

And yet Alder saw quickly that Wencil's teaching was more practical, more . . . well . . . *real* than Master Horto's. There were no ceremonies in his teaching, no complex formal exercises, no long dancelike routines, no elaborate drills, no arcane terminology. It was simple techniques, repeated over and over and over.

And over. And over. And then those techniques were tested in practical, hard, relentless sparring. Unlike at the academy, where sparring was discouraged as too dangerous, too undignified, too "unknightly."

Alder's shoulders hurt all the time. His feet were sore. His hands grew calloused. His arms and legs were covered with bruises.

But one day he caught a glimpse of himself in the mirror, and he realized that something had changed. His muscles were stronger. The layer of baby fat that had earned him so many cutting remarks at the academy had started to disappear. Even the shape of his face had subtly changed.

Each day as he dragged himself back to the castle, dirty and tired, he invariably ran into someone from the academy on the way home—often Eman or Neman. At which point he was sure to get teased.

"Nice stick. When are you going to get a real weapon?" "What are you and that crazy old man doing out there? Gathering flowers? Dancing with the fairies? Playing hide-and-seek?" The jokes went on and on.

Alder was too exhausted from his training to even reply. He simply shuffled back to his tiny, windowless cell in the castle, fell into bed, and slept.

One day Wencil said, "Why do you think they took advantage of you at the academy?"

"Because I didn't have any money?"

Wencil shook his head. "No. It was because you didn't take responsibility for yourself."

"What do you mean?"

"You showed up every day. You did as you were told.

But you left your destiny in the hands of others. You were being lazy."

"Lazy?" Alder spluttered. "But I worked hard. I did what they told me to!"

"It's possible to work hard, and yet be lazy."

Alder squinted, trying to puzzle out Wencil's meaning. Wencil came out with this sort of infuriatingly confusing statement all the time. "Well . . . how?"

"If you work hard doing the wrong job, is it really work? Or is it some kind of fakery?"

Alder didn't know what to say. He had never been one to question things very much.

"But . . . all the others had money! I didn't. So they made me work."

"They made you clean the floor and serve drinks because you let them."

Alder didn't understand.

"A Bedoowan knight doesn't prove himself when things are easy. You prove yourself when things are hard. The ipo tree grows in wet, sandy, bitter soil, soil that's too miserable for any other tree to grow. It grows slowly and painfully. Many ipo trees simply die and sink under the water. But the ones that make it? The ones that make it are stronger than any other tree. Because they have been tested."

Alder nodded. He was getting it now. Sort of.

"You are destined for something greater than this." Wencil pointed his gnarled cane at the castle. "These knights, they strut around, all puffed up with pride because they can tell a handful of Novans and Milago what to do. But this . . . this is nothing."

"What do you mean?" Alder had always been taught that the castle was the center of the universe, the most important place on the territory.

"You'll see," Wencil said. "There is a great struggle going on in Halla. You'll be part of it. But to play your part, you must be like the ipo tree."

"Halla? What's Halla?"

Wencil spread his arms wide, his cane in one hand. He swept them in a slow circle, taking in the river, the castle, the forest, the dark mouth of the glaze mine— seemingly taking in even the clouds and the suns and the distant, unseen stars. "This," Wencil said. "Halla is *all* this."

Alder looked around. He had never traveled more than a day's journey on horseback from the place they were standing. It was hard to take what Wencil was saying all that seriously.

"I just want to be a knight," Alder said.

Wencil laughed. "Of course you do. And for right now, there's no point in worrying about Halla."

"So when *will* I be ready to be a knight?" Alder said.

"Back in my day, you had to undergo an ordeal. A *true* ordeal. Now the ordeal is just a ritual."

At the academy every prospective knight had to go through what was called the "Grand Ordeal." It was not much of an ordeal though. You ran a gauntlet of the other students, who whacked you with padded sticks. The whole thing was over in about five seconds.

"What would a true ordeal be?" Alder said.

"Oh . . . I would say that going down into the glaze mines, finding a chamber marked with a star and retrieving a special ring—that would probably be the right test for you."

"The glaze mines! But everyone says Bedoowans die if they go into the mines for more than a few minutes!"

"Well, it wouldn't be much of an ordeal if you didn't put your life in danger, would it? Besides, that's just a tall tale"—Wencil frowned thoughtfully—"I believe."

Alder swallowed. Was he serious? It made Alder a little mad that Wencil was making fun of him.

"What if I went right this minute?" Alder said.

The old man shrugged as if he didn't care one way or the other.

"Okay! Fine!" Alder said. "I'm going."

He started walking down the path that led toward the mouth of the glaze mine. "Don't try to stop me! I'm really doing it! I'm going now!"

He kept hoping Wencil would stop him. He didn't really want to be poisoned to death in some dark mine. But Wencil just smiled and waved, then looked up at the sky as if he were wondering whether it might rain.

The path to the mine was about a mile or two long. Plenty of time for Wencil to catch up to him and tell him it was all just a joke. After a couple of minutes Alder paused and looked back. Wencil was nowhere to be seen.

Alder kept walking, as slowly as possible, pausing now and again, pretending to stretch or adjust his pants. But each time he snuck a look back—no Wencil.

And the dark, forbidding mouth of the mine drew closer and closer. There were a series of small hills on the way to the mine. Each time he came into one of the little valleys, he felt better. Plenty of time for this charade to end. And each time he crested a new rise, the black hole grew larger.

As he walked, he thought of all the stories he'd heard about the glaze mines. The Milago were undoubtedly inferior beings to Bedoowan knights, but they did have some kind of strange capacity to withstand the poisonous gases in the mine. Gases that could kill a Bedoowan in a heartbeat.

Or so they said anyway. No Bedoowan had been into a mine for generations. So who could say for certain?

While Alder was having these gloomy thoughts, he came over the final rise before reaching the mine. Alder was pleased to see that there was a small knot of young men standing between him and the mine entrance. They were doing something—though he couldn't make out what it was. *Maybe,* he thought, *whatever's happening here will give me a reason not to go into the mine.*

As he drew closer, Alder recognized two of the boys. His heart sank. It was Eman and Neman. He had been serving guard duty with them regularly. And they had used every opportunity to torment him. The third boy was obviously a Milago—he had dark hair and the pasty white skin that marked him as someone who spent much of his life underground.

Eman had the Milago boy by the collar of his grimy, threadbare shirt. Both he and Neman were much larger than the Milago boy.

"What were you doing sneaking around near the castle?" Eman was saying.

"I wasn't sneaking!" the boy said. "I was just gathering mushrooms for food!"

Eman pushed the boy into Neman. "Stealing the king's mushrooms?" Neman said. "Oh, that's a very serious crime." He shoved the boy back at Eman.

"Did you just shove me?" Eman said to the boy. "Neman, did you see that? This little Milago just intentionally bumped into a Bedoowan knight! I'm shocked!"

"Hey, guys," Alder said. "What's going on?"

Eman and Neman turned. Eman rolled his eyes. "Hey, look who's here!" he said with a big fake smile. "Thank goodness. We've caught a very dangerous Milago rebel, and we may need those scary fighting skills you've been picking up out there in the forest with Grandpa Wendy."

"Wencil," Alder said. "His name's Wencil."

Eman and Neman snickered.

"Whatever," Eman said. "Anyway, we got it under control, trainee."

Alder could have kept going. But the mine was scarier than Eman and Neman.

"Please," the Milago boy said, appealing to Alder. "I didn't do anything. I was picking mushrooms. Everybody in the village does it. There's no law against it."

"Is that true?" Alder said. "He was just picking mushrooms?"

Eman gave Alder a hard look. "I told you, trainee, we got it under control."

Eman punctuated his speech by giving the much smaller Milago boy a hard shove.

"I don't know," Alder said. "To me? Looks like you're just making trouble with the boy for no reason."

"Oh, really!" Neman said, smiling coldly. "Let me get this straight, Alder. Are you—a mere trainee—supporting a Milago, over two full-fledged Bedoowan knights?"

Alder cleared his throat. "I, uh . . ." He could feel his heart pounding in his chest. He thought back to all the speeches Wencil had given about how Bedoowan knights were supposed to be defenders of the poor. "Well, uh, yeah. I guess I'm saying I think you're just troubling this poor boy for no reason."

Eman looked at Neman. Neman looked at Eman. Their eyebrows went up comically. "Did I just hear the trainee correctly, Eman?"

"I believe you did, Neman!"

"Just let him go," Alder said firmly.

"You are joking, right?" Eman said.

Alder had always felt like his oversize body was a hindrance rather than a help in his quest to become a knight. But suddenly it occurred to him that he was by far the biggest of the four boys. He drew himself up to his full height. "I'm not joking. Let him go."

"Or what?" Neman said.

"Or else . . . *this*." Alder pulled the ipo stick from his belt.

Eman and Neman laughed derisively. "Hold the Milago," Eman said to Neman, "while I teach this weakling a lesson." He put his hand on the hilt of his sword.

Alder had the strangest feeling all of a sudden. It was as if he were watching himself. He would have expected to be scared. But he wasn't. He felt calm—almost eager. He had seen the training at the academy for years now, and he knew that it couldn't hold a candle to what Wencil had been teaching him in the forest. "Enough talking," Alder said.

Something flashed in Eman's eyes. Alder could see what was coming a mile away. It would be the standard gambit that Master Horto taught—a drawing cut, followed by a downward slash, and then a thrust. Alder put his left hand in his pocket. He was suddenly determined not just to beat Eman, but to make him look like a fool in the process.

Sure enough, Eman drew and cut. Alder sidestepped, the sword flashing by him. On the downward cut, he blocked. On the two thrusts that followed, he effortlessly parried. Eman paused, blinked, swallowed.

"What," Alder said. "That's all you got? I would have thought a full-fledged knight would be more impressive."

Eman forgot all about the standard fighting routines he'd learned from Master Horto. His face flushed with anger, he attacked Alder wildly, thrashing away. To Alder's surprise and satisfaction, he realized that Eman had nothing. Every move was awkward and predictable. He could see what Eman was going to do three moves in advance.

"All day," Alder said, easily parrying cut after cut. "All day."

"Little help here, Neman," Eman hissed from between clenched teeth.

"What about the Milago kid?"

"Forget about him!"

Neman quickly slid a rope around the boy's wrists, tying them behind his back. Then he lashed the rope around a tree, unsheathed his sword, and leaped forward. At which point, Alder realized he was overwhelmed. Eman was the big talker of the two. But it was clear within seconds that Neman was the superior swordsman. What had been an easy one-on-one fight suddenly turned into a two-on-one battle royal.

Fighting with his hand in his pocket wasn't going to hack it, that was for sure. Alder began fighting for all he was worth, using every trick that Wencil had taught him. But it wasn't quite enough. Alder saw that the Milago boy was furiously trying to free himself from the rope. With his hands tied behind his back, he was having no luck.

"Who's the smart guy now?" Eman said, slashing wickedly at Alder's leg. He was using the flat of his sword, not trying to cut him. Just trying to punish him. As Alder blocked the slashing blow, Neman stepped behind him and caught him with a hard rap on his back.

Alder whirled, caught Neman's elbow with a sharp blow. His blade went flying. But then Eman gave him another whack. That one stung!

As Alder turned his attention to Eman, Neman retrieved his sword. "Lucky shot, you big oaf," Neman said, whacking him in the leg.

Alder began retreating, a sinking feeling running through him. As he backpedaled, trying desperately to keep both Eman and Neman in front of him where he could fend them off, he saw a figure leaning against a nearby tree.

Relief flooded through him. It was Wencil. Good old Wencil would get him out of the jam!

"Wencil!" he called.

Wencil smiled broadly. "You're doing great, boy!" he called.

Doing great? Was Wencil joking?

Alder gave his instructor an imploring look. But the

old man just crossed his arms and continued to lean against the tree, a placid smile on his face.

Distracted by Wencil, Alder left himself open and several more blows caught him—one on the shin, one on the arm, and one nasty stinging blow across the face.

Alder realized that he wasn't going to win. That much was completely, painfully obvious. But he realized that if he was going to take a beating, at least he might achieve his goal of helping the Milago boy. If he could do that, then Eman and Neman would still have lost.

Alder reached into his belt, pulled his knife. With a flurry of blows, he managed to drive Eman and Neman back, opening just enough space to allow him to sprint toward the Milago boy. With a quick slash of his knife, he cut the boy free.

"Go!" he hissed.

The boy blinked. "Why did you—"

"Go!" Alder yelled it this time.

The boy didn't have to be told again. He turned and ran like a scared rabbit. And like a rabbit, he escaped by disappearing suddenly into a small hole in the ground.

Alder's focus on freeing the Milago boy, unfortunately, had put him in a bad position. Eman and Neman were now closing in on him from opposite directions. He couldn't fight them off both at once. Not without growing another pair of arms.

He decided it was time for a retreat.

It was then that his oversize body caught up with him. He had never had the steadiest feet in the world. So when his toe snagged on a root, he staggered and went down with a heavy thump.

Eman and Neman leaped forward, slapping him unmercifully with the flats of their swords. He had no option but to curl up in a ball and take it. The blows rained down on him from all sides.

Where is Wencil? he thought bitterly. *When's he finally going to intervene?* But as he snuck a glance at the tree where the old man had been leaning, the last shred of hope leached away. Wencil was gone.

"We'll quit," Eman said, "as soon as you admit we're stronger."

"Just say it, Milago-lover!" Neman added, whacking him hard in the arm. "'I'm a weakling.'"

"Weakling!" Eman said. "Weakling!"

Then a thin, clear voice cut through the air. "Over here, you Bedoowan creeps!"

Alder looked to where the voice was coming from. Now he saw it: The Milago boy's body was poking up from the hole in the earth. He was waving furiously.

"Over here!" the boy called again.

Alder still had his ipo stick gripped in his hand. He desperately swung it in a wide circle. Eman and Neman leaped back to avoid getting whacked in the shins. It gave Alder just enough time to stagger to his feet and start sprinting toward the hole where the Milago boy was.

"That's right!" Eman yelled. "Keep running, you chicken!"

Alder looked over his shoulder. Eman and Neman were trotting after him. Not rushing—but following fast enough that Alder knew he had no choice. Go down the hole or keep getting beaten.

"Follow me!" the Milago boy shouted.

Alder didn't have to think twice. Even though the idea of hiding in some overgrown rabbit hole didn't appeal to him, he couldn't stand the idea of any further humiliation. He dove into the hole. What the hole was, where it led, or why it was there—none of these question entered his mind. All he could think about was escape.

"This way!" the Milago boy whispered. The hole was deeper, larger, darker than Alder expected. Now that he was here, it occurred to him to wonder what kind of hole this was.

"What is this place?" Alder said.

But the Milago boy didn't answer. He simply disappeared from view, as though he'd fallen through a trapdoor.

Alder felt around blindly in the darkness. His hands closed around the rungs of what was obviously a ladder. So that was where the Milago boy had gone. Down the ladder.

"Weakling! Weakling!" Above him two sword points were probing into the hole. If he just sat there, Alder realized the points would soon be probing holes in his legs.

Without another thought Alder grabbed the ladder and descended into the darkness. After eight or ten rungs, he reached the bottom and found himself in a long tunnel lined with torches. The Milago boy was nowhere to be seen.

It was only then that he realized where he was.

I'm in the mines! he thought. *Now I'm going to die!*

Six

So," Wencil said, "you braved the mines, huh?"

Alder was lying on the floor in one of the back rooms of Wencil's house while Wencil rubbed salve into the bruises on his back and arms.

"I only stayed there for a minute or two," Alder said morosely. "When I came back up the hole, Eman and Neman were gone."

"So the fumes didn't kill you?" Wencil said with a knowing smirk.

"You think this whole thing is a big joke, don't you?" Alder said angrily.

Wencil slapped Alder on the shoulder, hitting him squarely on one of his bruises. "There. That should do it."

"Ow!" Alder said, pulling his shirt back on. Then he stood up. "Why didn't you help me?"

"You were doing fine," Wencil said.

"Doing *fine*! I was getting totally humiliated."

Wencil shrugged. "True."

Alder sighed. "So I guess they're right, huh? I'm just a big weakling."

"You stepped in to help somebody who was being unjustly attacked. You easily bested one fighter and then made a tactical retreat in the face of overwhelming odds. I'd call that a victory."

"Yeah, right," Alder said sourly.

"Look," Wencil said. "The reason you fought those two imposters to knighthood is because you wanted to help that Milago boy. In that you were successful. You *won*, Alder. You won!"

Alder cocked his head, curious. It hadn't occurred to him to think of it that way. "Really? You think so?"

Wencil nodded. "All these bruises? They're just trophies of your victory."

"I bet Eman and Neman don't see it that way. They'll tell everybody in the castle that they beat me." Alder contemplated all the jeers and laughter that would accompany him everywhere he went for the next few weeks. "How am I ever going to become a knight if everybody thinks I'm weak?"

Wencil stood and walked into the other room. "Come over here," he said.

Alder followed him. Like the rest of Wencil's house, it was barely furnished. Just a bleak, cheerless room that any senior Novan servant at the castle would have disdained to live in.

"Stand there." Wencil pointed at a spot on the floor in front of him.

Alder did as he was told.

Wencil drew his sword. "This blade is called 'Falling

Light.' It was forged in the great smithy of King Owenn. When King Owenn saw it swung, he said it moved like light falling from the sky."

Alder was feeling confused. What was this all about?

"Kneel," Wencil said.

"Huh?"

"Kneel."

Alder frowned, puzzled. Then he knelt.

"Are you ready?"

"For what?"

"To become a knight."

Alder felt a rush of confusion. Was Wencil making fun of him? Was this some kind of typical Wencil trickery, something designed to teach him yet another obscure lesson in knightly behavior?

"I asked you a question," Wencil said.

"Yes," Alder said. "I'm ready."

"Good." Wencil held out the sword. "This blade is now yours. Let it serve you well, as you serve others."

Alder took the blade. He felt numb and foolish and confused. He stared at the blade. Wencil had never drawn it, so he had never had a chance to study the blade before. It was the finest sword he'd ever seen. The handle was simple, worn with use. But the blade itself was extraordinary. Down the center ran a line of tiny runes, a legend carved into the steel in a language he didn't understand. But more important was the actual steel. There was a fine, wavy pattern in the grain of the steel, as though water were flowing beneath its surface. The metal seemed almost alive.

And in that moment, gazing at the sword, he realized that this was no joke, no ruse, no clever object lesson. This sword was real. Which meant . . .

"I—I don't understand—"

"Later this week I will go to the castle and enter your name in the registry of knights."

"But . . . you're supposed to have a big ceremony in court. It costs a lot of money. You have to have a certificate of completion from a licensed instructor. You have to—"

Wencil snorted. "King Karel was my student long, long ago. He will personally sign the certificate and the proclamation."

"*King Karel* was your student?"

"I must tell you, he was a mediocre student. But a very nice young man. Perhaps too nice to be a king."

Alder scratched his head. "You're really serious," he said. "About all of this?"

"Today people think that becoming a knight is an end. It's not. It's only a beginning. You are at the beginning of a long and difficult struggle. It used to be that a man became a knight on the battlefield. There was no ceremony, no chorus of trumpets. After a battle, after you'd buried the dead and packed away your weapons and fed your horse, a commander would approach you and say, 'You fought like a knight today. Now you are a knight.' And that was it."

Alder didn't know what to say.

"You fought like a knight today," Wencil said. "Stand up."

Alder stood.

Wencil took off the belt and scabbard that had held the sword, Falling Light, and buckled it around Alder's waist. "Now go home and rest. You've got a lot to learn, and we don't have much time. Tomorrow you'll need to train harder."

Train harder? Most Bedoowans pretty much stopped training the minute they got knighted. But instead he didn't say anything. Alder wanted to ask, *What's the point of becoming a knight if you're just going to train harder?*

Without another word Wencil turned and walked into the other room. Alder reflected how old and tired Wencil looked. After a moment he heard his teacher clumping slowly up the stairs to the room where he slept.

Alder stumbled out into the street. It was dark and the streets were empty. He hadn't gone more than fifty or a hundred yards before it finally hit him. He was going to be a knight! After all these years of anguish and fretting and embarrassment . . . There had been times when he'd almost thought it would never happen, that he would be one of those sad Bedoowans shuffling around the castle with no knighthood, the butt of endless jokes.

A warm glow spread through his entire body. A knight. A real knight.

He pulled out Wencil's sword—no, wait a minute, it was *his* sword now!—and waved it in the air. "I'm gonna be a knight!" he shouted, a huge smile covering his face. "I'm gonna be a knight!"

SEVEN

Wencil wasn't kidding. The next day was the hardest training Alder had ever had. Wencil made him run up and down hills, swim across the river and back three times, climb several tall trees—each exercise more fatiguing than the last. Then, when Alder felt that he was about to fall over, Wencil attacked him with a wooden pike.

For two hours they fought ceaselessly, wood thudding against wood. Sword against pike. Pike against short spear. Sword against sword. Short spear against staff. Staff against sword. There was no break for lunch. Wencil simply drove him harder. More running, more drills, more swordwork. Alder kept trying, his arms and legs growing more and more tired. But after a certain point, he just felt like he couldn't go any further.

"Why are you doing this?" he said finally. "Don't I get a break? Don't I get some kind of reward for becoming a knight?"

Wencil shook his head. "No," he said. "You don't."

Finally, when the suns started getting low in the sky,

Wencil sat down and leaned back against a tree. His face looked gray, his skin drawn, his cheeks hollow.

"Do you mind my asking how old you are?" Alder said.

Wencil smiled sadly. "Too old." Then he opened a small satchel and took out two apples and two pieces of bread. "Here." He handed one apple and one piece of bread to Alder. They ate in silence. Or, more accurately, Alder inhaled his food while Wencil picked at his bread. His eyes seemed dull, and he was staring off distractedly into the distance. Finally Wencil handed the rest of his food to Alder. "Take it, boy. I'm not really hungry."

Alder finished the rest of the meal.

When he was done, Wencil said, "I have some things to tell you. I may not have strength or time."

Alder looked at his teacher. "What do you mean?"

Wencil seemed uncharacteristically hesitant. "I had hoped I might call you 'son,'" Wencil said. "But circumstances prevented me from being here for you. I'm sorry for that. I'm sorry for what you've had to endure in this place." He waved his gnarled stick in the direction of the castle.

Son? What was he talking about? "I don't understand."

"You are not just a knight," Wencil said. "You are a Traveler. As am I."

"A Traveler? What do you mean?"

"That," said Wencil, "is a very long story. I'm not sure I have the strength to tell it to you tonight. Maybe tomorrow, okay?"

EiGHt

But the next day when Alder showed up at Wencil's house, Wencil was not there. A note was tacked on the door.

I am at the castle. I will have an audience with King Karel to discuss your impending knighthood. Don't think that I forgot about your ordeal. Today you must go into the mines and retrieve your ring. You must find a chamber with a star carved into the wall by the door. Inside you will find a ring that will mark you as a Traveler. Along with the ring, you will find your destiny. When you return, King Karel will affirm your knighthood.

—Wencil

Alder's heart sank. He'd hoped his fight the other day meant that he would be free from having to still endure the ordeal. Why couldn't Wencil have assigned him an ordeal like Master Horto did for his students at the academy? At the academy the Grand Ordeal was over in the blink of an eye. You got a couple of bruises and the whole thing was over. For a moment he wondered why he needed to go into the mines. What would it prove? It didn't seem fair. None of the other knights had to endure an ordeal like this.

But the feeling of resentment didn't last long. If Wencil wanted him to go into the mines, he'd go into the mines. Wencil kept telling him he was special, right? So now he was going to prove it! He smiled and began walking down the road toward the mines.

A few minutes later Alder was looking down into the hole where he had escaped from Eman and Neman the previous day. There was no marker, no railing, nothing to keep the unwary from stumbling in. He could feel his heart pounding. Ever since he was young, he'd heard how dangerous the mines were. Bedoowan kids were even told that there were monsters living in the mines. His Novan nurse, when he was little, used to say, "If you aren't a good boy, the quigs will come and drag you off to the mines."

He took two deep breaths, looked around to see if anyone was watching, then jumped into the hole.

Within two minutes he was down in the tunnel where he'd hidden from Eman and Neman. The torches on the wall threw a dim flickering light. The tunnel ran in two directions. Little trails of water ran down the rock walls. The air was close and chilly. Which way? He randomly chose to go to the left. After a minute or two of walking tentatively through the tunnel, he heard voices.

He began walking toward the sound. But as the voices grew louder, the tunnel grew darker and darker. Finally he could see nothing at all. He had to simply feel his way along the slick, wet rock.

Without warning, the floor gave way beneath him. He slipped and fell down an incline or chute, head over heels. Finally, with a sharp thump, he rolled out onto a solid rock floor. He found himself in a small, dimly lit cavern, its walls showing the marks of being carved by pickaxes. There was a hum of conversation around him.

He sat up and looked around. A group of Milago men were at work on the far end of the cavern, their bodies caked with grime, so that all that was visible of their faces was their white eyes. As soon as he sat up, the hum of speech ceased. Every miner in the room stared at him.

"Um, excuse me for interrupting," Alder said. "But I'm looking for a room down here. It's got a star chiseled into the rock near the door."

The miners stared at him as though he were a lunatic. Their eyes were not welcoming. In fact, they looked at him with undisguised hatred.

Finally one of the miners straightened up and walked toward him. "You're looking for a room?" the man said incredulously. There was something menacing in his voice.

"Yes. With a star chiseled next to it."

"A *room*!" The man grimaced. "We don't have rooms down here, Bedoowan."

Up on the surface Milago always looked at the ground when they were around Bedoowans. And they always referred to them as "sir" or "master" or even "my lord."

Alder felt a little annoyed at the man's disrespectful tone of voice.

"Well, a chamber? A space? I don't know what you call it."

The Milago man looked at the other miners. For a moment his teeth flashed. "A chamber! Well, then! Should we show him, lads?"

The cavern was silent.

The Milago man turned back to Alder. "No, Bedoowan, I don't think we will. Bedoowans aren't wanted down here."

"Now, listen here . . ." Alder tried to use the commanding tone of voice that Bedoowan knights normally used when addressing their social inferiors. But he thought it didn't really come out right.

"No, *you* listen here." The miner stuck his grimy finger in Alder's face. "You have no business here. Go back where you came from."

Alder stood up. He was going to try to show these Milago who was boss. But because he was taller than most of the Milago, he hit his head sharply on the ceiling. "Ow!" he said.

"Oh, loooooook!" one of the other Milago miners said in a mincing tone. "The poor clumsy knight hit his head!"

"Oops!" another shouted.

They all started standing, moving toward him. And they didn't look as if they were coming to help him. The miners all wore tiny lamps on their heads, the lights shining toward Alder, blinding him. He held up his hands, trying to block out the bright lights. What was wrong with these people? In the past he'd never heard

Milago talk like this. Not once. They were always quiet and respectful.

One of the miners lobbed a piece of rock gently toward him. It came so unexpectedly that it bounced off his face before he had a chance to move out of the way. The rock was big enough that it stung.

"Oops," the man who threw it said. "The silly knight hit himself again."

"You know, Bedoowan, mines are really not safe places," another miner said, picking up another piece of rock and hefting it in his hand. The rock was as big as his fist. "All kinds of accidents happen down here. Cave-ins, explosions"—his teeth appeared in the dim light as he smiled broadly—"falling rocks."

This time the miner hurled the rock as hard as he could. Alder dodged, but rock exploded as it hit the wall behind him, showering his face with sharp fragments. Alder felt his face. When he took his hand away, there was a red stain on his fingertips.

"Listen here," he said angrily, "I don't know what you people think you're doing but—"

"Payback time, Bedoowan!" one of the miners yelled.

Another rock whizzed by his head. Then another. He tried to dodge, but there were a lot of miners. And they were all throwing rocks. The rocks pummeled him in the chest and shoulders.

"What's wrong with you?" Alder shouted. "I never did anything to you!"

A rock hit him in the head so hard that he saw stars. Suddenly he felt terrified. If the miners kept it up, they could kill him!

As he covered his face and attempted to stumble toward one of the nearby tunnel entrances, a voice yelled, "Hey, guys, stop!"

The rocks continued to thump into him, and the miners continued to shout insults.

"Hey! Stop!"

For a moment the rocks ceased to hammer into him. Alder uncovered his face. He saw that a thin young miner had come into the cavern. "What's your problem, kid?" one of the other miners yelled at him.

"This knight helped me out the other day. He saved me from those two creeps who are always beating people up around here." The boy's face was so covered with grime that Alder didn't even recognize him.

"Who cares?" a miner shouted, hurling another rock at Alder. "One Bedoowan's no different from another. They're all leeches. All they do is steal our glaze and sit around up there in the castle getting fat."

"But *this* one's nice," the young miner said.

"Shut up, kid," an older miner said. "When you grow up, you'll see. Even when a Bedoowan pretends to be your friend, it's only because he wants something from you."

Several Milago threw rocks at Alder again. One of them caught him in the chest. Alder could see this situation was only going to get worse. It was time to run. He made a dash for the nearest tunnel.

"Not that way," the young miner yelled. "Follow me!"

Alder didn't have to be told twice. He dashed after the young miner, his head ducked low so he wouldn't hit the rough timbers holding up the ceiling. Rocks clattered off the wall behind him as he raced down the tunnel.

Jeers and angry shouts echoed through the tunnels. He could hear the men running after him.

"Get him!" the voices called behind him. "Kill the Bedoowan!"

Rocks thumped against the walls behind him.

"This way!" the Milago boy's voice called. The light disappeared to the left. Alder dodged into another tunnel. This one was so small and so dark he could barely make out where to put his feet.

"Shhh!" The Milago boy had stopped and put out his light. "Don't move," the boy whispered.

From the main tunnel behind them, Alder could hear angry shouting and footsteps. The two boys stood next to each other, frozen.

After a while the shouting died down. Finally the Milago boy relit his head lamp.

"Let's go back," Alder said finally.

The boy shook his head. "They'll be looking for us back there. We'll have to go out through one of the old tunnels."

Alder nodded. "Hey, look, thanks," Alder said. "My name's Alder."

"I'm Gaveth," the boy said.

Alder held out his hand. Gaveth looked at it for a moment, then shook it dubiously.

"Come on," Gaveth said. "Let's get you out of here."

"Actually," Alder said, "I'm looking for something. A chamber or room with a star carved in the rock next to it. Do you know where I'd find something like that?"

The boy turned and looked at Alder with curiosity. "Why?"

"There's something there that I need."

"Glaze?"

"No, not glaze."

"Then why would a Bedoowan come down here? Everybody knows Bedoowans don't come into the mines."

"I'm looking for a ring." Their footsteps echoed as they walked through the narrow corridor. The farther they walked, the thinner it got. Finally Alder was having to slide sideways through the narrow passage. The air seemed stuffier, hotter, danker, harder to breath. "Do you know where the room with the star is?"

Gaveth shook his head. "There are lots of tunnels down here. Nobody knows where all of it goes."

"Do you even know where we're going?"

There was a brief pause. "Not . . . uh . . . exactly."

They shuffled along for a while. "So, I heard there are quigs down here."

"Look, the mines can be dangerous. If you're careless. People tell all kinds of stories to try and scare kids so they won't wander around down here. But I've explored down here a lot. And I've never seen a quig."

"Oh. Okay."

Finally, just as the passage was narrowing to the point where Alder wasn't sure he'd be able to squeeze through it anymore, the passage opened up into a large cavern. Tiny points of blue light glittered from all corners of the big room.

"Whoa!"

"That's glaze," Gaveth said. "The main deposit here was all worked out years ago. But there are still tiny bits of it stuck in the walls."

Alder stopped and stared.

"We need to keep moving," Gaveth said nervously.

"Can't we take a break?" Alder's lungs were wheezing in the heavy, close air. "I'm not used to this air."

Gaveth shook his head. "No, we *really* need to keep moving."

"What's the rush?"

Gaveth pointed at the light on his head. "I've only got a limited supply of fuel for my lamp. There are no lights in the old sections of the mine. If you run out of light down here, you're in big trouble."

Alder didn't like this place at all. The darkness, the air, the claustrophobic feeling of the low ceilings and close walls. Just the thought of being down here with no lights gave him a sick feeling in the pit of his stomach.

"You know what?" Alder said. "Moving's good! Let's keep going."

They walked into another narrow passage. After a while it split in two. Gaveth stopped, hesitated.

"Which way?" Alder said.

"Uh . . . this way."

"You sure?"

Long pause. "*Pretty* sure."

"You're making me nervous," Alder said.

"Hey, do *you* want to lead?" Gaveth said, his face clouded.

"No. I just—"

"Okay then!"

Alder followed. "So, can I ask you a question?"

"I guess," Gaveth said.

"Why are all you guys so mad at us?"

"Mad at who?"

"Us. Bedoowans."

Gaveth seemed surprised. "Are you *serious*?"

Alder shrugged. "Well . . . sure."

Gaveth shook his head as though Alder had said something amazingly stupid. "You must be joking. Why would we *not* hate you?"

Alder felt puzzled. "Well . . . I mean, Bedoowans protect the Milago from invaders and bandits."

"Protect us!" Gaveth said scornfully. "Is that what they tell you up there in the castle? There hasn't been an invader or a bandit around here in generations!"

"Yeah, but that's just because we're ready at all times to fight them."

Gaveth laughed. "You Bedoowan live up there in luxury in your castle while us Milago work ourselves to death down here in the mines. Every year the king—or that nasty chancellor of his, Mallos—demands more glaze from us. Before Mallos showed up, it wasn't so bad. But now every year we have to dig harder and farther and deeper to find it. It's not fair. You know how many miners died down here last year?"

Alder shook his head.

"Dozens! And how many Bedoowan died defending us?"

"Uh . . ."

"If a miner gets hurt? Or dies in the mine? Guess what happens to his kids. They starve."

"Why doesn't anybody help them?"

"Have you ever seen a fat Milago?" Gaveth said. "We're all hungry. There's no extra food."

Alder couldn't believe it. All his life everybody had always said how the Bedoowans had it so tough putting their lives on the line to protect the Milago and the Novans. But Gaveth was right. Bedoowans hadn't been in any honest-to-goodness fights in, well, generations. Much less an actual battle. Or a war. So to a Milago, it probably looked as though the Bedoowans had things pretty easy.

And maybe they did. It made him feel strange to think that everything he'd been taught was a lie. He supposed that's what Wencil had been getting at, talking about "the old ways" all the time, about how the Bedoowans today didn't live the way they were supposed to. Alder had always thought Wencil just meant that Bedoowans had gotten lazy and didn't train hard anymore. But maybe Wencil had been getting at something deeper.

As everything that Gaveth said was sinking in, the two boys paused again. They had just entered a large cavern. There were six tunnels leading out of it. Gaveth kept looking from one to the next.

"Do you know where we are?" Alder said.

Gaveth didn't answer.

"Weren't we here about fifteen minutes ago?"

Gaveth cleared his throat nervously. "Maybe."

Alder suddenly felt as if he couldn't quite catch his breath. The walls seemed to be pressing in on him. All he wanted was to be out of the mine. "So . . . basically . . . you have no idea where we are."

"Basically? Yes."

Alder felt like crying. But knights didn't cry. "So which way?" he said.

"Uh . . ." Gaveth pointed at one tunnel entrance. Then at another. "This way?"

"You sure?"

For a moment Gaveth didn't say anything. Then they heard a rustling noise, a sound like something being dragged across the rock.

"What was *that*?" Gaveth said.

"You're the mine expert," Alder said. "You tell me."

Silence. Then two heavy thumps and a scraping sound.

Gaveth's eyes were wide. "Yeah, but you're the Bedoowan knight. You're trained for this. What should we do?"

"Um . . ." More scraping and thudding. It was getting closer and closer, louder and louder.

"Based on my training"—Alder heard his voice break into a higher register—"I think maybe we should . . ."

Alder spotted a pair of large yellow eyes gleaming somewhere deep in the tunnel.

"Run!"

Nine

Quig!" Gaveth shouted.

Alder frantically tried to draw his sword as the huge beast charged toward them. He couldn't see the quig. But he didn't need to. He knew what it looked like—quigs were giant bears with teeth as long and sharp as daggers, claws big enough to cut a man in half, and sharp spikes on their backs.

"Can you fight it off with your sword?" Gaveth shouted over his shoulder.

"Doubt it!" Alder yelled, finally freeing Falling Light from its scabbard.

The thumping of the quig's feet was growing closer. Gaveth turned hard right into another, smaller passage.

"What are we gonna do?"

"Try to find smaller tunnels!" Alder yelled back. "If we can get into a skinny enough passage, it'll get stuck."

"This way!" Gaveth dodged into another passage. This one was smaller still. The ground was littered with rock that had fallen from the ceiling. Alder stumbled. In the darkness it was impossible to see the floor well enough to avoid the dangerous rubble.

And still the quig kept coming. Alder could hear the sound of its claws rasping against the rock as it forced its way through the tight tunnels.

"It's definitely slowing down," Alder said. "But not enough."

"Here's an air vent." Gaveth's voice was high pitched and frightened as he pointed toward a rough hole in the ceiling. A wooden ladder led up into the hole. "Maybe this'll do it!"

Gaveth jumped onto the ladder and began climbing. Alder followed. As he clambered upward, Alder realized to his dismay that the wooden ladder was half rotten. Gaveth was so light that the ladder was holding him okay. But as big as Alder was, the wood was shifting and groaning with each step.

Wham!

The quig thudded into the bottom of the air shaft. Alder felt the entire ladder jerk. He tried to move faster.

Gaveth disappeared above him. He had reached the top. "Hurry!" Gaveth called, his forehead light appearing above Alder. Only a few more feet to go.

But the ladder was moving back and forth now. A terrible rotten-meat smell wafted up the shaft, carried by the rising air. Alder looked down. The quig was in the shaft now. It was crawling upward!

Alder couldn't believe something as big as the quig could get up the air shaft. But there it was, yellow eyes pinned on him, inching its way up the shaft.

Just as he reached the top, the rung that his bottom foot was on gave way. Alder's stomach rose into his chest as he plunged backward into the shaft.

He made a grab for the top rung, missed, grabbed the next rung and hung on, legs dangling into the darkness.

Snap! Snap! The quig's jaws were snapping shut.

Now this rung started to give way as well. Alder felt a flash of panic. He was done!

Then—just as the rung collapsed—he felt a hand lock around his wrist. It was Gaveth. For such a skinny kid, he sure was strong!

Gaveth lurched to the side, straddling the air shaft. "Hold on," he grunted.

"I'm holding! I'm holding!" Alder swung his feet around until he managed to get one foot over the lip of the shaft. From there he was able to push himself up.

"Thanks," Alder said weakly, gasping for breath.

"What now?" Gaveth said, peering down at the quig. It was still inching upward.

Alder pulled out Falling Light and stabbed down into the shaft. His first stab drew blood. The quig roared and thrashed, slipping back down a few feet.

"Yeah!" Gaveth shouted. "Poke him again!"

This time, though, when Alder stabbed at the huge beast, it batted the sword away.

Alder jabbed furiously. He managed to keep the quig from moving upward. But now he was having no success in drawing blood. And in the thick, unhealthy air of the mine, he knew he couldn't keep up this pace much longer.

"I don't—think—I can—stop it," he gasped.

"Then we've gotta run."

The passage they'd just entered wasn't small enough to slow the quig down. And, like the one below, it was littered with rocks, some of them big as Alder's head. It was obviously a very old part of the mine. The timbers holding up the ceiling were weak with age.

Alder continued to jab at the quig. "We'll never make it," he said.

"Wait!" Gaveth said. "I've got an idea. If we knock down the support beams, maybe we can cause a cave-in. That'll block off the tunnel and cut the quig off."

"Genius!" Alder said.

"There!" Gaveth pointed into the blackness. "That one looks like it's about to go already!"

Alder followed as Gaveth ran down the tunnel.

"Pull!" Gaveth grabbed the beam and heaved. Alder got behind him and yanked. The beam snapped like a toothpick. The two boys leaped backward, but nothing really happened. A thin trickle of dirt fell from the ceiling. But that was it.

Gaveth turned and looked back toward the air shaft. One of the quig's claws crept up over the lip of the shaft.

"Another one," Alder said. He slammed his shoulder into another support beam. This one wasn't as rotted as the other one though. "Help me."

Gaveth too leaned into the beam. With a loud groan, it finally gave way.

Again, the results were disappointing. A few pebbles fell from the ceiling. But nothing else.

Gaveth turned toward the air shaft again. The quig's snout had cleared the top of the shaft, and one muscular leg was hauling the big bear's body upward.

"We've got to run!" Gaveth said.

"No," Alder said. "Knocking down another support's our only chance."

"Come *on*!" Gaveth said. "Don't be stupid."

"It's this or nothing!" Alder said, putting his shoulder against the next support beam. "Trust me."

"Trust a Bedoowan?" Gaveth said. "I don't know."

For a second Alder thought he was joking. But he could see that the Milago boy was serious.

"Now!" Alder shouted.

"You don't have to yell," Gaveth said. He put his arms against the beam, braced himself, and heaved.

The beam slipped a little. But then it jammed on something and wouldn't move.

The quig was now clearing the rim of the shaft. In only seconds it would be on them.

"Never mind!" Alder shouted. "Run!"

They turned and ran with all their strength.

But they didn't get far. Alder's stomach sank as he saw what was in front of them. A blank wall.

"No!" Gaveth shouted. "No!" He pounded his fist against the rock.

Behind them there was a scraping noise and a thud. The two boys turned to look. The quig was in the tunnel now. Its flanks were heaving with the effort, and blood dripped in a steady stream from its nose, compliments of Alder's sword wound.

The quig was in no hurry now. Its yellow eyes were fixed on Alder, and the spikes on its back scraped the ceiling.

Scrape! Scrape! Scrape!

The only other thing Alder could hear was the sound of his heart.

The quig was even with the beam that Alder and Gaveth had been attempting to tear down.

Scrape!

One of its spikes lodged in a ceiling beam. The angered quig lunged forward to free itself. The support that Alder and Gaveth had been pulling on let out a sharp crack. The quig looked back in alarm.

The next thing Alder knew, there was an awful booming noise, like the ground itself was tearing in half. Then the ceiling came down with a noise that was louder and more terrible than thunder.

And just like that . . . the quig was gone! Nothing was left but a massive pile of black rock, and a choking cloud of dust.

Alder stared at Gaveth. Gaveth's eyes looked at Alder, big and round as gold coins. For a long moment, there was only silence.

"Whooooooo!" Gaveth shouted.

"We did it!" Alder rejoiced. "We killed it!"

They hugged each other and jumped up and down.

And then finally they stopped. Alder looked around. Suddenly his heart sank. Around them was nothing but rock.

"Uh . . . one question though," he said. They appeared to be trapped in solid rock. "Since you're a Milago expert in mining, tell me: How do we get out of here?"

Gaveth looked around. "I have no idea."

TEN

As the cloud of dust began to settle, Alder looked around. To his horror, he realized they were trapped. The rubble that had killed the quig had also trapped them in a chamber not much bigger than his bedroom back in the castle.

Gaveth met his eyes. "Uh-oh," Gaveth said.

"How long before the air runs out?" Alder said.

Gaveth shook his head. "Don't know. We'll have to dig our way out."

Alder looked at the pile of rubble. It rose clear to the ceiling. Some of the rocks in the pile were as big as Alder. Could they even *move* them? "What if it caves in more?"

Gaveth raised one eyebrow at Alder. "Then we'll die even faster."

"Sorry."

There was a long silence. It was the most silent silence Alder had ever experienced. As they stood there, afraid even to move, Gaveth's headlamp began to flicker.

"Oh, no," Gaveth said.

Alder could feel his legs and arms shaking. Every sense was heightened. A tiny pebble shifted and slid down the rubble pile. Shadows flickered and danced on the ceiling in the dying light of the lamp.

"So this is it, huh?" Gaveth said.

Alder felt a soft, cool jet of air against his face. It was strangely comforting, like feeling a gentle breeze on a beautiful spring day.

Suddenly something hit him. "You feel that breeze?" he said.

Gaveth shrugged morosely. But then his eyes widened. He smiled. "Wait . . ."

"It has to be coming from *somewhere*. Right? There must be a passage somewhere above us that the air's flowing from. Maybe instead of trying to dig sideways, we can go up."

Gaveth moved gingerly to his left. "The air's coming from this little crack right here," he said, pointing at a small dark hole between two boulders.

"Go," Alder said.

"Give me a boost."

The Milago boy took a deep breath, then eased himself upward and into the crack. Soon his torso had disappeared. Only his feet were hanging out. With the lamp up in the crack now, there was so little light that Alder could barely make them out.

The rock above them groaned. Dust sifted out into Alder's hair. *This place could come down any second,* he thought. Gaveth's feet disappeared.

Alder's heart began racing. The walls seemed to be pressing in again. He was completely encased in darkness. Utter, complete, total darkness.

He could hear Gaveth inching through the rock.

"I can see a tunnel!" Gaveth called.

"Can you make it?"

"I think so. Follow me!"

Alder climbed up into the tiny fissure in the rock. Gaveth had fit more easily. He had light, so he could see where he was going. And he was way smaller than Alder.

Sharp rocks poked into Alder's flesh as he inched forward. The space grew narrower. He rolled slightly and began crawling on his side. Inch by inch by painful inch he snaked forward. For a moment he was stuck. A panicky sensation ran through him. He squirmed wildly.

Suddenly the crack between the rocks widened slightly. Not much. But enough that he could use his hands again. He saw a light above him. A faint, flickering light. Gaveth was looking down at him!

"You're almost there, Alder!" Gaveth said. "Just a little more."

And then, finally, Alder was out. He lay gasping on the floor of a small tunnel. It was so low he'd have to crouch to get through it. But after the crevice he'd crawled through, it felt like the Great Hall of King Karel's castle. Relief flooded through him.

When he'd finally caught his breath, he said, "Don't suppose you have any idea where we are, Gaveth?"

"No," Gaveth said, looking around. His headlamp was flickering badly now. The narrow tunnel angled downward. Its walls seeped moisture, and the floor was slick.

"Hey," Alder said. "There's a light down here, Gaveth!" He began walking tentatively down the steep slope.

And with that, Alder's feet went out from under him, and he began to slide down the slope into the blackness. Without any light to illuminate handholds or timbers in the walls, he had no way of stopping himself. His arms and legs banged into the sharp rock walls, and for a moment he was sure he was going to be killed.

But then, with a hard thump, he came to rest on his back, staring straight up in the air. There was just enough illumination coming from an adjoining chamber to see a little. Alder looked up and blinked.

There, above his head, was a star carved into the wall. "We made it!" he shouted.

Suddenly a powerful light spilled from the adjoining chamber. The light was so bright and harsh that Alder could barely see. A man, his face and body visible only as a black silhouette in the darkness, leaped through the door. In his two hands, raised toward the ceiling, was a huge sword.

"Yahhhhhh!" the man screamed. Then he swung the sword at Alder's face.

ELEVEN

Caught off guard by the attacker, Alder was sure his skull was about to be split in half.

But just before the blade reached him, it stopped. There was a very brief pause, then the man with the sword stepped back into the light.

"Sorry about that," the man said. Now that he was completely visible, Alder saw that he was a tall, pleasant-looking man with a broad grin on his face. "When I heard all that thumping and bumping, I thought for sure you were a quig!" The man laughed as he sheathed his sword.

Alder sat up gingerly. After his undignified tumble down the steep tunnel, he felt like one giant bruise.

The smiling man reached out his hand. "My name's Press," he said. "If I'm not mistaken, you're Wencil's student, Alder."

Alder took the man's hand. Press effortlessly hoisted Alder to his feet. The man was dressed like a Bedoowan knight. But he wasn't anybody that Alder had ever seen at the castle.

Press looked up the incline into the tunnel. "Ah, that's young Gaveth, isn't it?"

"Do I know you?" Gaveth said.

"I knew your father," Press said. "Before he was killed in the mine."

Alder looked at Gaveth. "You? Your father . . . So, when you were talking about kids starving because—"

Gaveth looked away. "I'm old enough to work in the mine. We get by."

"Gaveth," Press said, "would you excuse us? I need to have a conversation with Alder."

Gaveth nodded. Alder followed the dark-haired man back into the chamber. It was illuminated by a brightly burning light of the sort used in the castle.

"Sit," Press said, indicating a hump of rock in the corner of the room.

Alder sat where the man pointed.

"I have a lot of things to tell you," he said. "But first, I've got something to give you." He extended his hand. In his palm lay a small silver ring with a stone in the center, its outer edge inscribed with tiny symbols written in a language that Alder didn't recognize.

He reached out and took the ring.

"What's this all about?" he said, trying on the ring. It fit perfectly on the fourth finger of his right hand.

"Like me," Press said, "you are a Traveler. Let me explain what that means. . . ."

TWELVE

It was late and dark when Alder passed through the walls and into the town that formed the outer ring of the castle. He stopped at Wencil's house. The house was dark, and no one answered when he knocked.

He continued on to the castle to go back to his dank little room. As he passed through the inner gate, one of the guards said, "Come with me, Alder. The king commands your presence."

Alder's eyes widened. For a moment he wasn't sure what the guard was talking about. The king? *The* king? King Karel? "You mean—"

But the guard turned away before Alder could finish his not-very-bright-sounding question. Alder flushed, feeling stupid now as he followed the guard.

They went through the entrance to the king's own household. Everywhere he looked, objects made from pure glaze gleamed in the subdued light. He had never been here before. The magnificence of the place was astounding.

Because it was late, the rooms were deserted. The only

sound was that of their footsteps.

Eventually the guard reached a heavy wooden door. He knocked, then threw the door open and said, "My lord, he is here."

Alder hesitated.

"Go!" the guard said harshly. "The king is waiting."

Alder entered. At the far end of the room he saw two figures standing next to a bed. One of them turned—an old man with a long white beard. It was King Karel.

Alder bowed low. "Your Highness," he said nervously.

"Come," the king said. He had bright blue eyes and a kind face.

Alder approached, recognizing the second man. It was Mallos, the king's chancellor. His face was cloaked in darkness, only one eye visible. It was a very pale blue.

"Your master is extremely sick," King Karel said.

It was only then that Alder saw Wencil lying on the bed. His face was drawn and haggard, and his eyes were closed. "Wencil!" Alder cried. "What happened?"

"Let him rest," Mallos said softly.

King Karel put his hand on Alder's shoulder. "Wencil was my instructor, you know. He was barely older than I. But he was the best swordsman alive." The king smiled sadly. "He was a great friend to me."

Mallos turned to Alder and said, "The king's doctor has been with him. He says that Wencil will not make it through the night."

"What!"

Mallos nodded. "Apparently, he had been sick for a very long time."

"But . . . he never told me. . . ." Alder felt a crushing weight on his shoulders. For the past six months—for the first time in his life—he had felt a sense of belonging, a sense of attachment. It was the feeling that everyone with a family must have, but that he had never really known.

And now . . . it was all being snatched away? It couldn't be! It just couldn't.

"I'm sorry," the king said. "I wanted to give my personal condolences to you. Wencil was a very picky instructor. He only chose to teach those of extraordinary promise. If he chose to teach you . . ." He spread his hands, as though nothing more needed to be said.

Extraordinary promise? From the way Wencil drove him, it seemed that he could never do enough, that he never had enough skill or bravery or talent. Surely there must be some mistake.

King Karel looked at his chancellor for a moment. "What do you think, Mallos? Is it time?"

Time for what? Alder wondered.

"While he still lives," Mallos said.

The king nodded thoughtfully. Then he turned to Alder. "Kneel, boy."

Alder felt confused. What was going on? But you didn't ask questions when the king told you to do something. He knelt.

The king drew his sword, a beautifully jeweled blade.

"Alder, pupil of Wencil, I bind you to the realm," he intoned. His voice was soft and scratchy. "With this, I call you . . . *knight*!"

Alder couldn't believe it. Right here? Right now?

A wave of relief and gratitude flooded through him. He had heard the words spoken as so many other boys became knights. And to think that the king was speaking them now . . . right here! In his own chambers!

With that, the king rapped Alder on each shoulder with the sword. Alder was surprised at how hard the king hit him. Each blow stung.

"Stand, knight," the king said.

Wencil stirred in the bed. Had he heard the ceremony? Had he felt a moment of pride that his last student had become a knight?

Alder felt tears running down his face. His mind was a whirl of emotion. His legs felt weak.

King Karel squeezed his shoulder. "I'm sorry, young knight. I would stay, but I am not so well myself." He smiled sadly and walked from the room. His gait was slow, and Alder saw that one of his hands shook uncontrollably.

Then the king was gone.

"An era is passing," Mallos said. "The time of great heros is slipping away, I'm afraid. King Karel and Wencil are the last of their breed."

Alder looked at the chancellor. He was an extremely tall man, thin lipped, without an ounce of extra fat. Unlike most Bedoowans, he looked like a true warrior.

For a while the chancellor was silent. Wencil drew in a long, deep breath. It sounded as if he were having to fight just to bring in air.

"Can't we do something?" Alder said. "Can't the doctors—"

"He's past that," Mallos said.

Wencil drew another long, ragged breath.

"Stay with him, Sir Alder," Mallos said. "He cared for you a great deal. As he slips away, let him know that you have understood what he has given you."

Mallos left without another word, leaving Alder in the darkness.

Thirteen

After Wencil's funeral, Alder felt aimless. He had nothing to do, other than meaningless guard duty at the castle gate. He had no friends. He had no one to train with. He was a knight now. But nobody cared.

As always, he remained cheerful, trying to be obliging, trying to be friendly. But it seemed to have no effect on anyone. He remained an outsider.

And the conversation he'd had with Press? It seemed distant and silly. All this talk about destiny and Halla and this big conflict between good and evil? Since that conversation, nothing had happened. He guarded gates through which no one entered the castle. He marched around the parade ground. So he was a Traveler. What did that even mean? The whole thing began to fade, almost seeming like some kind of dream. Or worse, like a cruel joke.

He felt as if he had been handed a brief moment of happiness. And now it was all being snatched away.

Then one day he returned to his room, and to his surprise, a man was sitting on his bed.

It was Mallos, black clad as always.

Alder stared at him.

"I apologize for invading your room," the chancellor said.

"No problem, my lord." Alder bowed. "Is there—did I do something wrong?"

Mallos's thin lips smiled briefly. Then the smile faded. The cold blue eyes studied him for a moment.

"I too know what it means to be alone," said Mallos. "To be without purpose and direction. To be without the bonds of friends and family."

"Sir?"

Mallos nodded. "Wencil was right, you know. You are a boy of extraordinary promise. I've had my eye on you."

Alder found this a little shocking. Other than the night Wencil died, he had never even spoken to the chancellor. "Really?"

Chancellor Mallos leaned toward Alder as if he were sharing a secret with him. "The knights here are mostly a useless bunch. But there are a few good ones. All the members of the king's guard are good men."

Alder couldn't figure out where this was going. Why was the king's chancellor sitting around talking about this in the room of a young man who'd been knighted not more than three weeks ago?

"How would you like to join them?" Mallos said. "You'd be under my personal command."

Alder stared.

Mallos smiled. "I'll take that as a 'yes.'" He

stood briskly and walked to the door. "Report to the guardroom at first light."

"Thank you, my lord!" Alder stammered.

The chancellor paused. "Remember, Sir Alder"—he touched the side of his nose with one long finger—"whatever you do, wherever you go, my eyes are on you."

And then the chancellor was gone. Alder paced around the room, a mixture of excitement and nervousness running through him like an electric charge. This was so unexpected that he didn't know what to make of it. The king's guard? They were the elite of the elite!

His head was in a whirl. Everything had changed so much lately. The king's guard, the death of Wencil, this whole Traveler business . . . and now the sudden attention of Mallos. It was hard to make sense of it all.

Alder had always heard bad things about Mallos. Cruel, mean, deceitful—all that sort of thing. And yet here he was, being really nice to Alder. Maybe Mallos wasn't so bad after all. Maybe he was just misunderstood. Maybe—Well, he'd find out eventually, wouldn't he?

HERE'S A SNEAK PEEK AT WHAT'S COMING
IN PENDRAGON: BEFORE THE WAR:

BOOK THREE OF THE TRAVELERS

The man fell hard, his face twisting in a grimace of pain as he thudded to the ground. His stick flew from his hand.

She ~~staff~~ .... her staff p... ed.
"Fall b.....................................

But...........

Lo.. nd.
She ex... But instead...........

Th.. ell.
There .... it were a signal.

With that, every one of the tribesmen released their arrows. The air around her literally whistled as the shafts came at her from all sides.

I have failed, she thought. *But at least I have died honorably.*

And then the arrows hit.

DON'T MISS THE REST OF LOOR'S STORY,
AS WELL AS THE STORIES OF PATRICK MAC AND
SIRY REMUDI, IN THE NEXT INSTALLMENT OF
PENDRAGON: BEFORE THE WAR,
ON SALE IN MARCH 2009!